I0539621

# ASSORTED
# SCOUNDRELS

Short stories, cynical and strange

Also by B. Mamatha:

*Keeping Lastly*
*The house they couldn't build*
*Bear-faced lies and other fictions*

B. Mamatha

# ASSORTED
# SCOUNDRELS

The Goldman Press

First published in 2017 by the Goldman Press

All rights reserved

© The Goldman Press

These stories are a work of fiction: the characters and events in them exist only in these pages and in the author's imagination.

No part of this publication may be reproduced, stored in or introduced into a retrieval system, or transmitted, in any form or by any means (electronic, mechanical, photocopying, recording or otherwise), without the prior written permission of the copyright owner, except by a reviewer who may quote brief passages in a review.

This book is sold subject to the condition that it shall not, by way of trade or otherwise, be lent, resold, hired out, or otherwise circulated without the publisher's prior consent in any form of binding or cover other than that in which it is published and without a similar condition including this condition being imposed on the subsequent publisher.

ISBN 978-0-9929394-7-2

Cover photo by Samuel Zeller on Unsplash

www.thegoldmanpress.co.uk

# CONTENTS

# The Burner Fallacy

Fred said he was going in the furnace. I said he had a gnat's chance – not of dying, because that was easy, but of making it out again. Either way, he was toast.

We were on a table by ourselves, Fred sitting across from me. The canteen – windowless, lights blazing – echoed to the scrape-scrape percussion of forks against plates. It was lunchtime but you wouldn't know it by its smell; you could barely tell it by its rations. The rest of our Cluster was spread across two tables close by, so I spoke quickly and quietly.

"Have a word with yourself," I was saying, but Fred had this look on face where he was smiling just in the eyes, like he'd made peace with it all. Maybe men like that were already dead on the inside. Maybe they shut themselves down in the hope that, when it happened, they wouldn't feel the sting of a thousand molten suns ignite in every orifice all at once.

"You got no chance," I said, "same as Parker or Symowitz, or any of them. What's your missus gonna do then? Your kids?"

A siren sounded in the distance and then, after a moment, closer by. One by one the sectors were screaming for their men, calling them back from lunch, back from the brink. We'd hang on until the last moment, for the final bell, though there was nothing to be gained in it either way.

Every day without fail the lunch special was a slop of grains, maggoty looking with the tang of wet paper, and even that was better than heading back to your station. So you ate slowly, chewed thoroughly, kept your eyes on your tray and your feet under the table.

"In the old days," I said to Fred, "when a fella died they put a coin on his eyes. To pay the ferryman; to carry him into hell. Dead men's wages: it's not worth that."

I snapped my fingers in his face and watched for the recoil but he just sat there, greasy in his boiler suit and strip lights winking along his scalp. I wanted to say something more, I wanted to convince him, but someone was in earshot. It was some guy – Dargeneau, something like that – ambling on by as though he had all the time in the world and not a care to spend it on.

By now the room was emptying, whole tables of men rising and turning in formation when their siren called. Only Dargeneau walked alone. I made a hill of grains and watched him shuffle one foot in front of the other, painfully slow and heading in the wrong direction. He was close enough to touch when he tripped and fell, then lay sprawled on the floor without moving.

To a man the Cluster faced forward, spooning air into open mouths. Getting drawn in was a mistake, but I could see the guy's foot lying beyond the edge of the table and gave it a tup.

"Don't be an idiot," I told him out of the corner of my mouth. Like Fred, he had no answer.

One of the guards came over. He took a gander at Dargeneau with the tip of his boot.

"Name and sector."

The rest of us dipped our heads, suddenly shy of the bright lights.

"Name and sector," the guard barked, and heeled the sleeping man in the ribs hard enough to roll him over.

Dargeneau had fallen on his fork. The front of his uniform was deep beetroot and damp, the blunt end of the fork just visible in the mound of flesh and mess. Dargeneau didn't move. No-one did. An alarm buzzed close by, hoarse and irritated: three-minute warning.

The guard toyed with a thin smirk. He heaved his foot back – pausing to adjust the angle – then kicked Dargeneau hard enough to send his boot burrowing as deep as the fork had gone. That did it; that brought him round. Dargeneau gasped and shuddered, face as red and damp and hypnotic as the spectre in his gut.

The guard blazed a full smile:

"Man down! Time violation. Send this layabout home."

That was it for Dargeneau. Not dead. Just dumb.

"I'm going in the burner," Fred muttered. "Tell the others."

I slid my tray to the end of the table, working myself into rage then tapering it off to a fine point. Men like Fred, dead like Fred, they had the easy way out. Going to see their families afterwards, paperwork in your pocket – that was the hard part. Watching their missus bringing up bile over a hand-me-down dress. Kids bawling by the bed. Flies on the meat. Maggots in the bin. Dead men's wages. Worthless.

"You." The guard's shadow fell across the table. "Walk this man off the lot, then get back to work. You'll be docked for your time. You can take it up with your fork buddy."

I bit back the burn and nodded. Fred watched me, eyes smiling vacantly. An alarm sounded overhead. Lunch was done.

The Plant was in Wapping, perched on the docks like a bilious toad belching sulphur and thick, noxious steam. It was a box-like building, a steel carcass about a mile long. Above ground were seven production floors teeming with men in identical get-up: grey overalls, soot in their limbs, quiet desperation. They walked without talking and worked without ceasing; they were the model of efficiency. Above the production floors you had your control rooms and the brains of the building. Up there was where the world was configured.

Just shy of five in the a.m. the sun rose somewhere beyond the sulphur and smoke. A crowd was massing at the lip of the compound, men pouring out of buses and then, as if dumbfounded by the dawn, falling silent where they stood. The reckless or the brass balled made at chit chat, asking after Jenny or Marie or Barbara or Helen. They listened in on rumours. They schemed and dreamed and smoked; they traded bargains to be had and connections to be made.

I dawdled by the perimeter, nodding at such-a-body and grimacing with the best of them, then wandered down the side of the compound. The building loomed beside me, cool and grey as the long shadows. There was a door down the way, almost invisible in the façade yet, like my knowledge of the sun, I knew it to be there. It was the service route: it bypassed the working floors with their production lines of machinery and men, and terminated five floors below ground.

Down in the bowels incinerator level was a grid of corridors, each one a half-mile tube punctured at regular intervals by metal doors. Those were your furnaces: 20-foot concrete rooms laced with pipes and jets and latticed grills for the run-off.

If you were on burner duty you were assigned a furnace and that was your lot for the day. You waited for the gurneys to wheel up, five or six at a time stacked high with machine parts and motherboards, paper still wound on its spool, metal cabinets, boxes of gears. Rumour was that everything went to furnace in the end.

Each man was a master of logistics, a brute force automaton. Everything was unloaded by hand and heaved into the furnace, where it was re-stacked in perfect configuration down to the last cog and washer – and all to time. The furnaces all fired at precisely the same moment; their bells and whistles and slamming doors were mechanised for precision.

Once the firing bell rang each man would stand down momentarily, by grace of the Company, and start figuring for the next load. It was fast work if you didn't want to lose an arm – or worse. But you grew to moving to its tune, the body pounding rhythmically while the brain wandered free. So a man had time to muse, and that's when some of them got to thinking.

See, if you were paid, you were lucky. For most it was food stamps. In the right circles there was cash, or what was left of it after dues. To work was a privilege, and wages were a loan from the Company – and they clawed it all back, bit by bit, through dues: Uniform Allowance, Transport Stipend, Nourishment. And then there was your lottery stake: Insurance.

If you died in service, your insurance paid out. The money was meant to cover a regulation plot and a cardboard casket, but most families had an agreement: use it for food, smokes, anything to make living a little less punitive. Death, they figured, was an easy sleep all things considered.

The big money wasn't in dying, though, but in slicing it thin. Get injured badly enough and you'd get that nominal payout for the remainder of your no-good life, year-in, year-out. We didn't know anyone who'd pulled it off but we heard plenty plan it out. We even helped carry some of them out afterwards, or what was left of them.

The problem was the margin was too tight for any man to slip through. Like Dargeneau, for instance. After a mishap – that's what they called it on the paperwork – if a man was on his feet and walking, he wasn't dead. If he made it across the compound and through the gate he was done for. Once he crossed the line he was on his own: whether he was crippled for life or bled to death in the parking lot, his insurance didn't count for Jack.

That was the get-out clause – that was the bind. Unless you were obliterated on Company property, or came close enough that they couldn't just walk you off the lot, the chance of your family seeing any cash was non-existent. It was a stacked game, and it was the men working the furnaces who figured to beat the system.

Say your uniform catches on the side of a crate or you're moiling at the back of the burner and the first alarm sounds: that's doors closing. Your brain sums the dimensions of the room even before your feet are moving. When the door slides shut it's a wonder of engineering, heavy and seamless and swift.

Then you're in there, lights out and sweating. Bang on the door with your spanner. Somewhere in back you hear the gasp of ignition and you realise how hot it is. The air's baked – there's no time to cool between firings. The atoms are fried and there's nothing left to breathe.

There's a window in the door as big as your hand, the glass about an inch thick. It's scratched to hell, but suddenly you see things clearer than ever: the corridor is silent, but there are men moving not a foot away from where you're stood. They're dancing, or so it seems, twirling stacks of paper and metal cupboards, smooth and in slow motion like they're moving through hot wax. They can't hear you, and you can't hear them, because everything's roaring, and you don't know if it's the furnace sparking into life, or your guts racing to evacuate. The window's pitted and marred, and only now do you think to count how many of those dents have been made by someone else's spanner – and still you bang and you scream.

The second alarm's the firing bell. The jets come on in sequence at the back of the room; yellow flames as long as pool cues. When they all fire the temperature jumps from residual heat to over 5,000 degrees in about 90 seconds. At best you've got 15.

You've got your palms pressed against the window because you can't watch the world leave you behind. The soles of your shoes are smoking. It's too hot to cry, or to breathe. Somehow the furnace has infiltrated you; the heat's in your lungs and you're exhaling smoke. You've got your eyes closed but you can smell them cook. The only thing you can do now is stay upright; stay standing like the man you are; because when you go down you won't bake – you'll flash fry.

There's a split-second lull – a hurricane's eye of silence in which you're floating. You hear the door seals suck themselves tighter for impact. 15 seconds becomes 20, becomes 25. If you're lucky, you don't make it to 30.

Sum it out like that and you see it for what it is: a 15-second window that can spin dying into an eternity. Those dumb enough to dream it figured those 15 seconds could be squeezed razor thin. You had your cluster, your compadres; you moved in unison and sweated out the day together. Enough men working together was a battery of brute force. Enough fingers wrenching the door from its seals could over-ride the operative and snatch you back from the brink. It was just a matter of timing.

Fred lived north of the river. On a clear day Plant-side you'd say you could see his place and as far as Wanstead, but it was a lie. You couldn't see past the smog and steel chimneys, or you just never thought to look for the horizon.

Up close there was no loss in it. Fred had rent on two rooms split between front and back of a house on Sarter Street. It was one of those fake-fronted streets: bay windows that never caught the light, doors ripped off the hinges and balanced on their posts, damp crawling up partition walls. His missus was a mousy woman, buck-toothed, or so she seemed – it might have been the illusion of her emaciated face. The power was off but she offered me a drink anyway. I swallowed it cold and watched her draw her teeth back behind her lips.

"How you bearing up?" I asked.

She looked away and into a corner, speculating for renovation. The place was grimy even with the curtains drawn, as though she could never quite scrub it clean. The kids were leaning against a bed in the back room; two of them, both boys. They didn't look like Fred. They didn't look like Connie either. They looked like rats, shaved in the head and grubby in the face, with dark, darting eyes.

"Wary you?"

Connie had an odour to her, pungent enough to bring the water to your eyes. There was a collection of knick-knacks balanced on a shelf behind her; plaster people with fancy skirts and chipped faces.

"What?"

"Were you with him?"

Soft lilt to her accent and the way she moved, as if not quite up to the task. She circled the room, hands bunched in the pockets of her dress. It was maybe June around that time but she was wearing socks inside her slippers, and a blue cardigan that had frayed away at the sleeves. She looked down at me, terrifying in her skin and languor.

"Were you there when it happened?"

I considered the question from afar, as though it had all been weeks or years ago instead of days and hours. "No," I said.

People lie for different reasons, and I hold no grudge or gavel for it. Some lies come about because there's no imagination for anything else. Sometimes it's for kindness, but mostly it's because the truth is never clean.

Sure we could have reminisced, me and Connie. How Fred had told me he was going in the burner but that it took months before we got called up for it. I could have said how he'd unpicked the pattern of the bells and timed it out, dawdling at the back of the furnace until the last moment; how he'd bailed almost immediately and hammered to come out.

I could have sung the tune of men throwing down tools and swarming in the corridor like they were running for freedom; how they'd flocked about the burner, prising at the door seals, hands on hands, backs against thighs against arms and faces.

I could have run the calculation of the tipping point: that it takes 12 men's hands to breach the seal – not a digit more, not a digit less. How the door had creaked on its bolts like it was for turning and a last gasp of hot breath had blown through the crack. And then how at the final moment the over-ride switch had blinked red, and the mechanism snapped shut on itself like a well-oiled bolt. How? It wasn't for the knowing, hers or mine.

Connie circled the kitchen table, daintily stepping her heels across the ripped carpet. I lay a hand in my pocket and kept it there still as a mouse.

"He told me that morning, he said, 'I'll be seeing you'. That was the last thing he said. It was dark out still. I didn't even open my eyes."

She screwed her eyes shut where she was standing, then opened them and regarded me balefully.

"That is the thing of it," I said, feeling the folded paper square in my pocket.

"I don't know what to do, how to be."

"No."

My fingers slipped inside the crease and teased it open against the warm lining.

"It's like falling, I tell you that. It's the queerest thing."

She drew a chair to the table and sat for a moment, quite prim.

11

"It's like we can't remember already. We just want to know or hear. To say."

She snaked an arm across the table and drew a finger in the dust.

It was mid-day, silent but for a handful of flies sizzling on the windowsill and the younger kid bawling in the bedroom. He was still young enough to cry; he was that age when crying is still a reflex, like breathing or blinking. He and his brother were a matching pair. They'd been cut from a pattern, down to the yellow shorts and bare feet. They were thin-limbed and pot bellied, eating themselves from the inside out. My fingers stroked the cheque, summing the weight of the ink against this bare-bones life.

Connie's hand strained across the table, palm turned up towards me.

"Won't you stay? A while? Stay." She looked me full in the face then glanced away as if overcome.

I got up slowly, watching the shadows in the bedroom. They were standing, the two boys, like they'd been constructed but never switched on. Their arms hung down loosely past the tops of their shorts, but the older one held his fists clenched. I caught his gaze. He was a rivet in the making.

"Of course," I spoke the lie slowly, "I'll come back soon."

She'd already drifted away from the table, picking at her fingers like she was remembering a ditty. She wouldn't turn around, but her voice crept after me.

"Is there anything for us?"

I had my hand on the door, fingers grasping for the handle.

"Fred walked out. He made it to the gate. He said … he asked for you."

Afterwards I stood on the landing and picked at splinters in the wall. I listened to the sounds floating inside – a gentle crooning and then a clattering, as though something had fallen from a great height.

I straightened my jacket and raked my fingers through my hair. I would carry the cheque away still in my pocket and burn it. Not out of bad-mindedness, but because Connie had boys, and I couldn't pay them to stay hungry; because there'd come a time when it wouldn't always be like this – they wouldn't always be children. The older one would stay lean and starving, and he would grow a piston where his heart had formed. The boy becomes the man. The man becomes the bullet. What I knew of the world told me it was as true as the sun rising without fail and setting unseen. It was just a matter of timing.

The afternoon street was hot under its canopy of smog. There was noise and dust from trucks ferrying their goods, but the people had disappeared, hiding away in holes or summoned back to toil.

A little way past the aqueduct there was a scrolling screen fixed high above the rooftops, a mechical banner floating against the impenetrable sky. It reported the weather in pixelated type, a never-ceasing roll of good news to be taken on trust.

'28 – high! UV – high! Sunny' and then, as if to labour the point, a row of yellow suns.

# *Man Buntu*

It was lunchtime, and Buntu was looking for me. Noon couldn't come as far as the storeroom, which was dark and cold and pooling with rain water, so we fixed our faces in squinting grimaces as though we each held the other responsible.

"A man is outside," Buntu announced.

"So? Open the shop, bring him in!"

"He's not that type of man."

"Oh? Is he a woman?"

Buntu was a small, leathery boy the colour of a roasted nut. He had a curious slant to his mouth so that he always appeared scowling. He was a taciturn fellow; I believe that's what I liked about him.

He gave me a look of disdain:

"It's not a customer."

I went to see for myself, peeping through the window at the front of the shop. Buntu climbed up on the counter to watch me, making great art of chewing something in the side of his cheek – as though he were the proprietor and I his good-for-nothing shop boy.

The man lying motionless on the verandah was a stick figure, with long limbs folded beneath him like a grasshopper. He'd arranged himself in a plain white shroud – part bedding, part daily wear, very economical.

"Sleeping?"

Buntu merely shrugged in response, so we fell to silent contemplation of the man-figment.

March is rainy season, when the water falls from the sky and forms new rivers, warm and blood red like the hills they pass along the way. The dirt road outside was flooded and would remain so for days, perhaps weeks, but below his shroud the sleeping fellow was shoeless, feet as rough as jute. He was red-skinned up to his ankles, but his natural colour was honeyed. His hair was grey turning to silver, particularly in the beard. He was so thin as to be an amazement. I could see the joints of his skull in his face.

Buntu wiped the counter with a dry rag. He worked in slow movements, the cloth whispering like a prompt. I fetched the key from the hook myself but took my time opening the door.

"Ai," I called from the threshold.

The sky was translucent, carrying with it that smell of earth and copper as it does after rain. The porch was wet. The wood was soaked and the water would carry around the foundations and into the storeroom, where the rice would slowly ruin.

Up and down the road the town was gone. When I had first come to that place it was a bustling thoroughfare – greasy litter, peanut shells, petrol-laced. It was an industrial junction, but every day the loggers cleared a little further east until eventually they simply belonged to some other place, and the townsfolk followed after them.

"Ai! What are you doing here, old man?"

"Ask him, ask him," Buntu murmured.

"Fetch the broom."

Buntu brought it sullenly, as he did everything sullenly. I brushed the old man lightly, dusting the broom over his red feet. Beneath the lids his pupils were watery and grey.

"Why are you sleeping here?"

The old man mumbled.

"One hundred years old," Buntu whispered.

"Where did you come from?"

Pesaquoia, the stranger said. Pesaquoia, easily a day on foot for a younger man. That was all he could say in our tongue. Instead he rocked his hands: 'Let me sleep', he seemed to gesture, 'I'm tired. Go inside and let me take rest'. It was a marvel – that he could be so eloquent without words.

Buntu hovered in the doorway as though now, after all this time, he had the gift of rhetoric. I pulled him inside and shut the door, and he glared up at me bullishly.

"Shut up," I said, though he hadn't spoken. "Fetch your books."

Buntu stood on one leg to regard me. He wore the same clothes every day – an American T-shirt and greasy shorts – but he carried himself like a tiny businessman. He shook his head slowly, as though I was barely worth the trouble.

"And so why, Mr Big Shot?"

"Mistake," he replied.

"And what do you know about it?"

"Others will come." He fixed me with a look reserved for one who doesn't know the customs of your place.

"Others who? You're talking nonsense. He's an old man. He could be your grandfather." I said this to Buntu, who had only a mother. "Is it a favour to let an old man sleep on the floor, to stay out of the rain?"

Buntu cocked his head as though hearing hoards of vagrants already marching on the mountain road.

"What have I given him? If a man asks for nothing, can I say no?" I considered this for a moment. "Buntu, everybody expects you to grow into a big man, but the more I hear from you, the more you're like an old woman."

I threatened him with the broom handle but he wouldn't cower.

"Fetch your books. You old crow!"

There was little else to do after that. Who was left to come to the shop? Sometimes farmers, but it turned out they could live off cattle and crops. Plastic packets of machine parts ordered years ago disintegrated. I stored the parts in a box on a high shelf above tinned goods and intimates. All grew dusty together.

Buntu was young enough for school, but there was no school. His mother thought he might learn a trade from me but there was no trade either, so I ordered books. That's how we idled away the afternoons, in the pursuit of knowledge as shining and elusive as the rainbow.

"What do you think, Buntu? Will you get your certificate?"

He shrugged.

"If you don't have any education, what will you do? You'll be like our friend out there."

He sat up straight, appearing for once to hear me.

"You could get a good job, have a better life. You could earn money for yourself, for your family."

Buntu looked around as though seeing the shop with renewed interest. After a moment he fired his shot:

"You don't pay."

I laid the book on the counter, pressing it flat until the spine cracked. "And you barely work."

He smiled to himself as though I'd handed him a candy.

"Then go home," I said. "Did these books fall out of the sky? Where do they come from?"

Buntu swivelled his eyes in his head until they came to rest on the boxes disintegrating on the top shelf. He looked up there, then down at me, conveying the full intent of his insolence without so much as a word.

"When you're educated –" I grabbed his collar "– when you come on time, leave on time – when you do a useful day's labour – come then. We'll talk."

He pushed me away as though he tired of me. His collar had ripped. It lay against his throat like a necklace.

"My mother learned you more than you ever learned me."

I wondered what his mother would make of it, this grown man squeezing her son like a lunatic. I smoothed his shirt regretfully.

"Your mother is a wise woman."

"She told you. No one else did."

"Yes, she told me. Who has money for machine parts, when they can cut a plough from a tree, or strip a truck for its metal? You're a resourceful people. You live in the soil and you call it home.

"Your mother is a smart woman. Perhaps I should have hired her instead. But I didn't, and so – who knows – perhaps my debt is paid."

He looked at me, curious.

"What debt?"

"Always big questions, Buntu. Why can't you do what I ask you? If I can't pay you, I can teach you. Why won't you learn?"

"Why you let that man sleep there?"

"What business is it of yours if I do? If I do a kindness for someone, why do you take it for an insult?"

"No customers come now. But if they come and the beggar is there, they'll go away. Then other beggars will come. Then no customers at all. Only beggars."

"It's nonsense, Buntu," I said saldy, "you're thinking the wrong thing."

I patted his shoulder reassuringly.

"That old man will be gone by tonight. You'll see."

"Others will come."

"Then I suggest you read your lessons thoroughly, unless you want to join them."

It was resolved; I had been clear on the matter. Later I cooked, slitting a bag of rice and watching the portion turn thick under its milk skin. When I ladled out three bowls, Buntu put his hand on mine firmly, like so.

"Why?"

I thought about the old man, blade-limbed, arm so thin I could have circled it between finger and thumb.

"Sometimes you leave scraps for dogs, don't you?"

Buntu didn't reply. He leaned across the stove, one hand protecting his shirt from the flame, and fired a bullet of spit into the third bowl.

I felt no fury for that portion. I thought about the rice rotting in wet sacks, a bounty we couldn't sell and which was too big for the both of us.

I set the bowl down carefully, wiped my hand on the side of my trousers, and slapped him. If he felt the blow or understood its meaning he wouldn't show it. I hit him again for impudence. He regarded me flatly, no tears for crying; no words.

If Buntu was a stone under my heel, the stranger was a boulder of another kind. He lodged on the verandah, motionless while the days circled in on themselves. Sometimes he disappeared in the middle of the day, only to return with the dusk. He said nothing, ate nothing; only draped out his cloth, placed one arm over his face like a blindfold, and slept. I watched the road for other rags on the horizon and the waiting was a punishment.

Then a number of things happened. They came in a rush, falling quickly one after the other, as though each belonged to the previous. One morning there were two bodies in front of the shop, each wound in their bleached sheets. The second man was middle-aged, as thin as the first but with a full head of black hair. He was more forward – he treated the verandah as his personal compound, coughing and ejecting wads of phlegm over the side of the railing.

I fretted in the back of the shop. Buntu was no help; he was under my feet like a rat, always chewing something or nothing in the side of his cheek. When I couldn't bear him any longer I put him to work in the storeroom and locked the door after him. He was quiet a while and then I heard him scuttling here and there, rattling the shelves and causing the rice to whisper in its sacks.

"What are you doing, you rascal? I'll come in there!"

He grew quiet and I left him to it. It was better to bear the sound of him than see his face. I unpacked a radio from its box and flooded the shop with tinny jazz, with trumpets and voices sliding up and down their harmonies.

Later, when I unlocked the door and looked, Buntu was sitting quietly on a throne of rice sacks. I picked a path through the mud and wagged a finger in his face.

"If you've been making mischief…!"

He was tired, and answered in a sleepy voice: "I helped you, boss. I'm only helping you."

He patted the rice sack fondly, and I could see he'd raised several bags on blocks of stones and broken bricks. He showed me his hands – they were like clay plates.

"I found these bricks just floating, boss."

20

Each rice sack was as large as Buntu, and easily twice as heavy. The bricks he'd used to raise them above the thin tide were like peanuts supporting an elephant. It was a circus illusion: charming, but of no practical use.

Buntu was sleeping on his feet. I pulled him out of the back room, wiped his hands and gave him the handy-sack of rice I used to store our portions: "Give it to your mother."

I steered him onto the verandah and past the blanket bodies. The moon was coming up in a cloudless sky; the world was picked out in milky sheen. Buntu stroked the cloth bag, bouncing it in his hands as if weighing the price for himself.

"Don't leave it somewhere!" I rapped his sleepy head.

He gave me a half-lidded stare and left without a word, speculating something keenly on the road as he went.

In the morning, everyone had disappeared. I inspected the verandah and it was the same as it had ever been except the men were gone – their berths were empty and a row of coins lay instead on the window sill. It had rained all night: footprints and scent were washed away, but those coins had seen the city and the coastline; they'd skirted the flat lands and climbed the backbone of hills to the west. They weren't enough for a bowl of tea, but I put them in the drawer and locked it.

I looked out on the road – not for the vagrants, who had gone the way of the loggers, but for Buntu. I watched for him until noon crept around the door, then ate alone.

The day stayed wet. The downpour was so heavy, so unceasing, that part of the storeroom floor broke free and slid away under the far wall. I hitched up my trousers and waded in after it. I clawed the mud for the broken parts, then gave up and watched the water reclaim the grains.

After some time I heard Buntu come into the shop. I heard him catch the door with his hand so that it wouldn't bang, and waited in the passage as he crept about. I'd intended to leap out suddenly, to make him jump and whinny, but the boy standing there was frightening – stained in scarlet where the mountain road had clung to his clothes, and where he was bleeding.

His face was swollen on the left, one eye almost disappeared beneath the cheek. He stood in front of me, drenched and small, somehow, but with his fists curled in front of him.

It was as hard to speak as it was to look at him.

"Who did this to you, Buntu?"

He kept his chin firm, always the little businessman.

"Where have you been? Who did this to you? Did someone bring you here?"

There was a curtain of daylight at the window but outside the street was empty.

"Are you hurt?" When I gripped his shoulders he was shaking.

He mumbled something tuneful.

"Shall I take you to your mother – why didn't you go home?" I paused. "What soldiers?"

"By the water tank."

He tried to scowl from his bloated face but it just seemed that he was winking. Then he walked slowly to the counter and vomited.

There was no sense to be had; just a yawning pit of fear that threatened to swallow the shop, the road, and everything. I cleaned the counter with one eye turned on the window. The clouds slipped across the sky in yellow-hemmed skirts. Then the clouds sailed on and the sun threw red after them. The world turned on.

"What soldiers, Buntu?"

He tutted. "There are soldiers, a camp. You don't know. You don't go out from your shop."

"Why were you there?"

Buntu puffed out his chest.

"I always go there."

It was a revelation, heavy like a falling pillar.

"Why?"

He looked around the shop in answer.

"You want to be a soldier? Dirty and uneducated and –" I couldn't say the rest, not to a child. "Then what? Why did they stop you?"

"I was talking with them," he said, as though he had words to hold counsel with cockroaches, never mind grown men.

"They did this?"

He peered into some dark corner of the room.

"When did soldiers come here? What do they look like?"

"Big," he said, and tried to duck behind the counter. I caught him with my foot.

"Why did they beat you?"

"They want money. They say I have money. I tell them no, but they don't believe me."

I threw my hands up; I wanted to rip my hair out in handfuls.

"Big men! Brave soldiers!"

I unlocked the money drawer and tipped out the contents. Buntu blinked slowly with an eye and a half when I pushed the coins into his hand. I had one arm around his neck. He was slippery to the touch in his wet skin and clothes. His twisted, sideways gaze was frightening.

"Come! They want it; let them take it."

He struggled out of my grasp.

"No," he said firmly while his shoulders quivered.

"Don't you see, Buntu? Don't you see – it's not right. It's not right! Even rats can do what's right."

I pressed a coin against his palm.

"That old man had nothing – he took nothing – yet even he left a portion. I'm ashamed for myself, when I think. Ashamed. What could you know? What do you know of the world? You're a boy. You don't even know your books."

Buntu set his face as though he knew something of the world and would never reveal it. The dirty coin lay on the edge of the counter where he'd thrown it and his swollen eye kept turning toward it.

I picked up the coin and turned it over in my hand like a wonder.

"What have you done, Buntu?"

He looked away, a gaze deep enough to pick out husks in the distant fields.

"Where did the old man go? Just like that, he left – why?"

"Don't know," Buntu muttered. He made a sudden movement, turning to point at me with a gun-like arm.

"You said. He put his money and went. Why are you asking me?"

I slapped his arm away so hard that he was blown back on his feet. We faced each other with war expressions.

"What trade have you made?"

A furtive look passed over his face, as though I'd spied on him at toilet.

"Trade? What does it mean?"

"What have you done you cockroach, you snake? You told your soldiers about the men."

"No."

"Yes. Whose blood is it on your clothes?" I squeezed his face until his swollen eye bulged. "How could you do it, Buntu?"

"I did nothing! Liar. You're a crazy.'

He was pushing me away with all his strength. I reached past him easily and grabbed his shirt, the logging company logo a red sun under my fingers. His chest was rising and falling, rising and falling. The T-shirt tore just as I held it, straight up and down.

We sprang apart and watched each other, Buntu's shirt open like a waistcoat. Underneath he was sleek, like coal held under water. He regarded me knowingly, his bloodshot eye unblinking.

"They ask me for money because I told them one time before, I say –" his voice was high, almost crying, but not. He took a deep breath, sucking in air and dust and the endless day.

"I say I work in my father's shop."

He took a step backward; quiet now, measured. He moved to the door which had stood open the whole time. He stood as high as the bolt notch. Behind him was grey sky, rain. He pulled off the remains of his shirt and let it slide to the floor. He stood straight backed, ribs sharp against his skin, nubs of muscle like spring buds. Then he turned on his heels and was gone. I watched him running along the road, skittish and light, like litter caught on the wind. He was twelve years old.

I believe I saw Buntu on one other occasion after that day. It was on the train to DeMer. I travelled in a first-class carriage with a straw bag and a flask under my seat. Every compartment was full but the faces changed from station to station: families with tied parcels; an old man with a bicycle; schoolgirls in matching plaits and ribbons.

Once I woke with a start and thought I saw him sitting opposite me – Buntu, but expanded to six feet tall. He was as dark as ever, but his complexion had fitted to him like a suit. He was wearing a thin-striped shirt and long leather shoes. He looked to have done well for himself.

I watched him from behind my newspaper, wondering if there was a more fitting epithet for our kind of friendship. He regarded me briefly, then fixed his gaze on the landscape hanging between the window bars. His body moved in time to the jolting tracks like a well practised dance.

I was just setting the words in my mouth when his eyes darted towards me; he had straightened in his seat.

"Perhaps you remember me." I faltered and he studied my words without speaking. The train crept on, and on.

"Perhaps you remember me," I said, the sentiment falling like rusted bolts.

He didn't reply, and then suddenly was standing over me. The top of his head almost grazed the metal fan bowls screwed into the ceiling. He gave a broad smile.

"I'm afraid not."

He tipped his hat at me and reached quickly for his case. From the window I saw him leap onto the platform while the train was still crawling in. The dust jumped up to meet him, and bare-chested boys ran after him like a bridegroom's party. He leaped with them, their voices falling together in the open air like he belonged to them, or they to him. Then he sped on, along the platform and under an arch and onto the open road. The boys sang him on his way, crowing and skittering and chasing at scraps until they forgot him and turned back to their game.

# Curdle Sight

The daddy would come to her room in the small hours, when the house was dark and the mother sleeping downstairs. It was a wooden house, with a gnarly flank of Johns Pine standing between it and the mountain. Everything – home, trees, hill – was given to the creaks, so the daddy would climb the stairs softly in well-worn boots.

The world glimpsed through an upstairs window was an unblinking eye of black and white halves. If he could have flown up among the stars he would have seen the homestead lying desolate between the mountain and the sea, and not a body but the three of them for miles.

The boots were given to pause then at the lip of the stair, as if summing the weight of yet another descent. And then, with a sigh, the daddy turned back, to a door at the end of the hall.

It opened to a narrow room under the slope of the house, with space for a bed and a wash stand. The wash stand was crooked, and there was a doll-haired child asleep in the bed. The thin blanket was dusted with snow – there were fine cracks in the roof – but the girl's arms lay above the sheet because she was bandaged from finger tips to elbows. Beneath the vinegar strips she was burnt and crisp, and the room smelled at once bitter and sweet.

The daddy pulled off his boots, tipping dirt by the door where it couldn't be seen in the dark, and wouldn't be noticed in the daylight.

"Are y'asleepin'?" he asked in his lullaby voice.

Jennet's breath was soft and even.

"Are y'asleepin'?"

Before, when not bound in vinegar strips, Jennet would wrap her arms around the daddy's neck. He would tell her how it was to build a railway to the coast. In the cities they were building up into the diamond sky but out here they dug down, blasting away as though somehow they knew a steel road ran true beneath it all.

He would tell the miracle of the railroad burrowing out of the ground like an inchworm, and how men rode alongside in an open wagon, twenty of them at a time. How they carried cakes of explosive compound on the way out, and on the way back, crates of men – or the pieces of them. He said what it was like to glimpse the sea or hear immigrant songs for the first time; how those wild men worked the mud like they belonged to it.

Jennet was silent. Eyes closed, she dreamed of floating among larch tops. She was carried up the mountain by a cradle of warm air, yet when she looked down her footprints followed behind in the snow. She stirred uneasily.

"Da?"

The daddy was remembering the wild tunes and rolling a terrible sadness inside him. It was a fine thing they built for pennies a day, all blackened together, burdened together, burned together. He remembered himself and grunted a reply.

He got into the bed, then helped Jennet to lay back against him, he the pillow. He cradled her and ran his hands over her hair. The moon spied them through the window and, as it sank below the sill for the last time, picked them out in brilliant, fleeting glare – and was gone.

In the sudden dark the daddy was frightened. He pushed the girl away and half-fell, half-floated to his feet.

"Our father ..."

His throat was dry and the words crumbled.

"Our father ..."

Jennet gripped the bedsheets as best she could.

"What is it?"

"Hallowed be thy name!"

"What is it?" she cried.

He mumbled. He groaned. He was a shapeless apparition in the black.

"Get thee behind me, Satan – thou art an offence unto me!"

"Da," whispering now, "you're scaring me."

He found her shoulder and twisted it.

"How've you done it? How've you made the devil's work?"

She hid her face in the pillow.

"What work, Da?"

There was a long-time scratching, and then he'd lit a lamp and was standing over her. He was a patchwork of deep shadow and red, like the woodcut in the family Bible.

Jennet lay shivering face-down as he parted her hair this way and that and raked his fingers across her scalp. She imagined she could see him looming above her; he had the look of a man panning for gold in a boiling river. The heat from the lamp seemed close by, buttery against the sheets, and then it withdrew to some far, far corner of the room.

She waited for him to call it for a jest, but he merely groaned as he bent to fasten his boots. He stepped into the hall, and then there came a new noise: as he closed the door, he locked it.

The sky was edged with the red and gold wings of dawn, if it would only come. The wind moved above the house and whistled through the cracks like a breakfast kettle. Jennet fetched the lamp and sat close to it, shrinking away from the edges of the room and the shadows under the bed. She watched the promise of day forming in the wash stand mirror.

After some time she reached for a looking glass, forming a fist around the handle until the pain of it drove her dizzy. She parted her hair just as the daddy had, and angled the two mirrors.

She turned this way and that, glimpsing wefts of hair and then the dawn, then strands and knots, then scalp and broken skin, and then, buried beneath it all a wound of sorts. It was as wide as the tip of her thumb and bruised purple. The hair around it had broken short and rough; it resembled a small pocket of sewn flesh. She touched it. It was numb, like no part of her, and then the wound shuddered and opened of its own volition.

The hand mirror clattered blind on its face – but not without first showing its gift. Doubled back and forth in the glass the wound had peeled open like a bud. Inside, looking back at her, was an eye.


Day turned to night turned to day turned to darkness. The daddy came back some time in between and nailed boards across the window. He worked fast, and wouldn't whistle as he usually did. He tied a night cap on Jennet's head and fastened the ribbon in a cascade of knots. It was tight enough for choking.

The mother fussed around the edges of the room fetching bread, taking away the bucket. She was a willowy woman with a face made for pious joy now turned ashen. She wanted to examine Jennet for herself.

"What is it you need to see? Didn't I tell you clear enough?"

"Maybe –"

The daddy stood beside her weighing the hammer in his hand and she put the thought away. She stole a look at the child when his back was turned.

"I have to change the bandages."

"Don't touch her."

"But she's ill!"

"The devil has strong hands. You're not to touch her, not to come here alone."

She drew iron from deep in her gut to speak.

"Suffer little children to come unto me."

"Aye," he admitted, but when she stepped toward the bed he caught her by the neck – "You'll mind what I say!" – and pulled her from the room.

After they'd gone it seemed desperate quiet, hushed enough to hear hens scratching in the yard, or geese wings moving in formation high overhead.

At first there was a game to fill the hours; Slumber Dog, whom she imagined at the foot of the bed. Jennet could hear him snoring, a sometimes-noise like hunger, or water bubbling on the stove. If she was quiet – didn't move, didn't make a peep – the dog would stay asleepin'. If she cried she'd wake him, and he'd be mean and angry for it. He had red eyes and red teeth, and he would find her by her squirming and eat her. It was a game of little comfort.

It was noon when the mother crept back. The daylight she carried in from the passage was already so unfamiliar that at first she seemed all sun and no substance, like an angel.

"Jennet?"

She took a step into the room.

"Your daddy's away."

Another step.

"Jennet?"

"Yes."

"We won't tell him I came."

A wave of nausea – unexpected, like bugs in the flour sack – caused her to stumble. There was an overwhelming odour about the girl, sweet and rotting. The bandages were damp. She tried to unpick them but Jennet twisted out of reach.

"Don't be stubborn, girl."

Jennet glanced at the door. "He'll know."

"Nonsense."

"He hates me."

The mother gave some thought to the matter.

"A man set out on a journey during a blizzard. It snowed so hard that you couldn't see your hand in front of your face.

"But the man wouldn't be defeated: he walked and he walked and he walked. He walked for such a long time that when he finally stopped, he didn't know where he'd come to. Everything was white. He couldn't see anything of his home town. *Ach*, he said," – and she made the accent, dredging it up from the old country, lyrical and rolling – "*Ach, I'll just live here.*"

"Is daddy lost?"

"Of course not! He hasn't stopped praying for you. You remember that." She looked fierce, then smiled. "Why not eat something? I'll help you. Aren't you hungry?"

Jennet shook her head, but it was a lie: hunger stretched along her bones and shuddered when she breathed. It was pin pricks in her chest, and needles in the palms of her hands.

"What if ..." Jennet's voice was small.

"Yes?"

"What if the devil is me!"

The mother tutted.

"Just let me see what's going on under there!"

They tussled for the bonnet.

"Show me," the mother threatened, "or do you want to grow old in this room?"

She jerked at the ribbon, slicing her fingernails through the knots. The night cap was flung aside. She pulled the girl's head low as if combing for lice. After a moment she straightened up and grew still watching cracks of sunlight inch across the bed.

"Well! I thought I'd find horns under there. Or the devil's sum."

A range of expressions flitted across her face and, as if knowing it, she tapped her foot quickly on the floor.

"Why, there's nothing there!"

She straightened the bedclothes, moving around the room carefully.

"But your daddy was so certain. I wonder how that came about?"

Jennet shrugged. "Don't know," she said. "Don't know."

The mother dawdled at the foot of the bed, tugging at some nugget of curiosity. The moment passed. The talisman night cap was folded away into the pocket of her apron. She closed the door and locked it, and her footsteps pattered away.

Jennet was asleep, but it seemed that some part of her mind was awake and hovering above the pillow. Pale morning seeped past the boarded window, picking out the room in dusty outline. Her earthly possessions were stacked on the wash stand: a hairbrush, a locket, an ivory comb once owned by a China princess. Eyes closed and dreaming, yet Jennet saw all quite clearly.

There was a noise at the door and the daddy came in wearing his Sunday suit, Bible in hand. His face was pale, eyes blinking and watery as though it were he that emerged from a hole. It wasn't until he was standing over her that she realised he was weeping. It was a curdling sight.

Jennet jolted awake. There was the room. There was the window behind its board curtain, there the basin. There was light in one corner, and shadows along the walls. The daddy was sitting close to the bed. He was wearing his Sunday suit and mulling the Book of Job.

He placed a hand on her arm:

"There's nothing to be frightened of."

The daddy read on, following the words with his finger and the shape of his mouth. Jennet turned away to face the wall, her breath soon soft and regular once more, and he closed the book and wound down the flame. He stood and knocked the stiffness out of his knees. When the girl didn't stir he reached for a pitcher – cream coloured with blue flowers: dense and pretty. He held it above the bed, inching it higher until it hung there like an undecided moon. He felt its weight and trajectory, felt it move, willed it so – and then the child woke.

Jennet slid out of bed and turned on her heels to face him, all in the same deft movement. She had a curious look on her face, or what he could see of it: placid in her brow, furious in the eyes. Her lips were stretched in half grin, half shock.

The pitcher fell short. It landed on the pillow then rolled onto the floor, where it split into three broad pieces plus splinters. Man and child watched each other from across the room, breath rising and falling, rising and falling.

The yard was empty, chalk outline of hop-along vanished under a crust of snow. Even the hens had withdrawn to their coop, heads drawn into their breasts as though their necks were snapped.

Jennet passed by in a blur, racing ahead while her new eye showed her what was left behind: grim house, dirt tracks spoiling the pristine ground where the wagon had rolled away.

The mother had appeared in the doorway while the pitcher still rocked in pieces. Are you coming to church, she'd asked. Her eyes refused to rest on the scene. Aye, the daddy said, and clasped the book against his chest.

A few minutes later the mother returned alone. She placed Jennet's boots against the wall without a word, and closed the door so gently that it merely kissed the latch. But when the moment came there was no time for boots or cape. There was only heart and breath and bare feet skittering on ice.

Jennet flew beneath the pines, a tenebrous path that opened into flat expanse of diamond snow. Across the plain, under the milk sky, and onto the rising mountain – she ran.

At first the way was sharp with rock shards. Then the slope evened and there was moss on the forest floor. Down on the plain it was hard winter but autumn had stalled on the hill and the trees clung to their colours.

The bandages had unfurled and trailed after her, red and yellow streamers. She flung them off and examined the crackled coating beneath. Some of it could be lifted clean off in whole continents and underneath skin had formed, fresh and intact.

She flipped her hands and inspected the new wounds, a mottled line stretching the length of each palm. She drew a finger along the ridges and her bones answered with a dull vibration. The wounds trembled, but stayed shut.

There was no sound except heart and breath. Slowly she calmed and other noises emerged. A solitary crow looping its ugly song among the branches. There was water close by, and a dog in the distance barking for coming storms. She grew uneasy and set off, winding once more against the face of the mountain.

The daddy was behind, not yet in sight but gaining: Jennet's hollow footprints stretched across the snow calling out the way. He lost her at the edge of the plain and pulled his hat up on his head to survey the horizon. The route opened up at the base of the mountain in bent twigs and bloodied toe marks and he was on his way, rising into the clouds and low-drawn heaven.

His boots were sturdy on the rock and he outpaced her. They drew level in Willow's Dread, a wide basin of damp earth with an open face of sheer-sided granite. Ahead lay sky and the plains, soft and white and – from such a height – seemingly perfect.

"Where are you going?" he asked her, straight and true.

Jennet pointed out and over the clouds. The daddy stepped into the clearing.

"Stop this. You mind me, now! Stand back from there."

"Why?"

He was puzzled. "Why?" He thrust his hands in his pockets and stamped his feet. His breath rose and fell and froze in crystals in his beard.

"You've been ill. You had a fever so high, and there was nothing we could do about it. Nothing."

"I fell. I was burned on the stove."

"Yes, you fell and burned yourself. We didn't know you were sick until then. I carried you to bed myself. You remember."

She tried. She picked over the bones of recent memory and found nothing new.

The daddy took another step.

"I know what you're doing," she blurted.

"What's that?" He was closer now.

"You want me to fall."

He looked her over and laughed.

"You're ill," he said. "You've a sickness in your head."

Jennet glanced over the edge. The side of the mountain was like a fresh-struck gem, jagged in parts but slippery.

She was struck by a sudden dread.

"Where's ma?"

He was close enough to grab her. His boots dug into the dirt and she flailed about him like string. They teetered on the brink, the world spinning and the white plains sliding in and out of view. They fell backwards – not into the void, but away from it. They rolled and came to rest in the Dread.

A chill wind moved across the mountain. The trees bristled and shook their foliage, golden semaphores in the cloudy day.

Man and child lay still, faces and beard and breath pressed up against each other. The daddy's pocket had split and his pistol had fallen out. He was unfussed by her looking.

"I always carry a gun. You know that."

It was true; he said you couldn't trust the land or any creature on it, and that was the way of the world.

"Why not your rifle?"

"There wasn't time to pack a picnic either. I came quickly."

"Can't hide a rifle in your coat."

"No. But with a rifle I can shoot a doe before she even knows I'm there."

It was an impasse. For every question there was an answer, well fitted, if not believable. The wondering grew stale. They faced each other while the mountain turned on, imperceptibly, beneath them.

The daddy retrieved the gun and stepped to the edge of the clearing. He snicked the hammer with his thumb and aimed it at her. Jennet didn't move. They were connected by an invisible line, father and gun and girl.

The daddy's face was pale when he lowered his arm. His hand shook and he seemed sick when he said, "Is it enough? I could have done it, if I'd wanted."

Jennet hesitated before going to him. She climbed his body, face against beard, arms around neck. He smelled of pepper and soot. The thought came to her that he may have been inclined to shoot, but by the shaking of his hand he would have missed. She felt his arm rising behind her, and thought she saw it too, clear as the day. He had the pistol upside down, butt travelling towards the crown of her head.

She cried out – it was more frustration than fear – that this was a game for grown-ups. Her arms clamped around his neck and he groaned for the sudden stoppage of air. The thin-lipped ridges in Jennet's palms burst open and inside were not eyes, but rows of teeth, tiny and moist and toxic They reared out of their casing and sank into his neck, his face, his ears. They punctured him over and over – toy bites, neat and painless.

He dropped her where he stood and watched the low sun with an awestruck expression. He stumbled on his feet and went down, falling among the tree roots and soil.

Jennet moved quickly. She skirted the clearing and vanished into the trees. She didn't stop; didn't look back to see he lay where he had fallen. He would still be there when she rose along the spine of the hills; she would cross the limits of the land while he petrified slowly from the inside out. That she wouldn't see, yet she knew she'd done a terrible thing, and she ran the faster for it.

The trees were dappled, growing dim. The sun was shrinking and soon it would be dark, and dirt and long worms would climb out of the ground and cling to her. There were bears in the forest, and wild cats as big as steamer trunks, and no place for her among people. There was no turning back; she had her own kind of protection now. It was a game of little comfort.

# *After the Wake*

The dog came in a box. He told himself he'd bought it because it was on sale, but once home it seemed a futile thing.

It was a kit of 150 pieces. Metal struts and hinge joints. Lubricated sliders, wiring in yellow casing. Cavities which could be fastened together. A pair of plastic eyeballs. The heart of it was a compartment about the size of your palm: a neat housing for electrical impulses, for software and jewelled circuits. That was the sum of the thing.

He worked in the living room to the tune of a clock echoing in the kitchen. The day was a mask of shadows along the walls and then the carpet and, finally, in just one spot behind the door.

When it was done, it was ugly: the shape of a dog without the detail. Knee-high and gun-metal grey, wiring congealing inside the frame. Its absences were unnerving, and the face was wrong.

He switched it on and ran through basic commands. Begging was menacing, a rearing up on the hind legs. Stay was redundant.

"We used to have one of these. Well, my son did." Bernie Williamson's wife called in sometimes; she liked to swivel her eyes around the front room. She stroked the sideboard and smiled: "They don't last long."

She straightened photo frames and fiddled with a patchwork elephant collapsed on its trunk. "Why not get a real one?"

Mrs Williamson watched him clear up, screwdrivers and Allen keys piling on the coffee table. They didn't talk, and soon his face was burning. He excused himself to go to the bathroom and stayed there until he heard her leave. Finally he came back and regarded the afternoon's work.

The fabric hide was misshapen and ill-fitting. The effect was something like starvation, the dog sunken and rattling in its skin. He discarded it and sliced the fur trims from a cape in the closet instead. He brought the sewing machine down from the attic and read the instructions. The new skin was barely better than the first and ripped where the joints flexed. His third attempt was passable.

Days passed and the job engrossed him. He prised out the eyeballs and replaced them with glass ones, whittling the stalks for superior motion. He swapped the sheet metal components with alloys, soldering on the dining table and dripping oil across the lino. He fitted bellows which inflated the chest at indiscernible intervals. He tapped his screwdriver across the circuit board, touching this contact and that until the joints bent fluidly, silently.

The dog was named on the box as Castor but the creature in the living room grew feminine in its new frame. He toasted her with tap water and called her Birdie.

Late in March he left the house. He looped a belt around Birdie's neck and to that attached a length of cord, and then they walked – across the road and around the houses and into the park. Birdie was too neatly programmed. She didn't pull at the leash, or rear up at cats or cars. She didn't want to be free. He strategically torched her circuits and upgraded her chip and, slowly, sentience began in the eyes.

At first she was constrained to mimicry but gradually grew to react in her own way. Sometimes he would hide upstairs and call her. Mostly Birdie ignored him, and that was OK. Later she came as far as the bottom step, head turned towards the darkness and scanning the silence. Finally he stepped out from the playroom and saw her tail raise in recognition – but she just stood there, one foot on the step, waiting for his word.

Spring brought pride and its failings. The former took place in Notman's, near the school. Notman in his grey cardi and cataracts, was bent over a stack of newspapers:

"Oi. No mutts."

Birdie was leaning against his leg, cold like an iron bar, and yet it seemed a triumph. "You mean her?"

Notman looked up, lips twisted, face twisted, dead-straight in his meaning.

Afterwards they walked the long way. They crossed the suburbs and out onto the country's edge, Birdie veering to inspect the dust and the hedgerows. Rooks screamed from the pylons. Dormice floated in the furrows.

They were halfway to Garton, about 4 miles from home. The water came softly, and he turned his face up to greet it. Drizzle turned to a fine-weft shower and he spiked his collar; by the time his hair curled sleek across his jaw it was too late. It was raining.

He tugged the lead and they started back the way they'd come, then stopped and ducked beneath a flattened bank of firs. He tucked Birdie under his jumper, manoeuvring her until her nose nudged out just below his chin Her eyes were open, eyelids fused in place. Without moving parts she was a lump to be carried home in the crook of his arm.

The brown fur was ruined. He unpicked it and draped it in front of the fire, but it warped and shrank as it dried. He unpacked the hair dryer from a trunk and ran it over the dog's inner workings. Repeatedly he'd stop and try the switch, but she just lay there, C-shaped, synthetic tongue lolling around the hinge in her jaw.

Birdie stayed on the carpet in pieces and he took to eating in the kitchen once more. Mrs Williamson felt vindicated.

Summer was ending before he picked up at it again. Birdie was rusting in her crevices, and he scraped away the worst of it and oiled her over. He attached a thin heating mechanism to a new hide, and polished her ball bearings. The computer was ruined and had to be replaced, and then reprogrammed. Sit. Come. Think. Strain. Flee.

He was lying in bed one night, listening to the sound of her bellows soft against the sheet. Birdie was warm on his foot, and heavy, and he nudged her without meaning to. She gave a muffled snort and then, from some hidden consciousness, rearranged herself. He placed his hand close by her and clucked. Eyes still closed, she heard him and shifted closer.

He continued dining in the kitchen – potatoes or cheese; milk from a plastic beaker. He walked Birdie twice a day until monotony set in. The dog knew him, and followed him from room to room regardless, tail weaving behind her. He kept her dry where he could, and sometimes he couldn't, and she grew musty and wasn't allowed on the bed any more.

He came to going out without her, and she waited in the front room with her head on her paws. At first she howled, and then the parts wore down and she grew wheezy. He stepped over her, nudging her against the wall so he could carry the sewing machine to the bin out back. He brought her box down, too, then left it in a corner to grow a spider's web on its lip.

"Maybe," he told the dog, and she looked at him with her head on one side. She came over, stiff in her joints, and placed a paw on his knee. Her fur was bunched golden under her neck as though they'd been playing at buttercups. She furrowed her brow and watched him awhile, then pushed her nose against his fingers.

"Maybe," he wondered aloud. He shrugged her off, then dropped a hand on her head; smooth ball of skull and machinery. He petted her until her tail twitched, then he carried her upstairs and lay on the bed beside her.

"There now. You go to sleep."

He waited until the sound of her bellows hushed, the familiar weight on his leg. Crooning in the dark, he called her Castor.

# *Meta Variations*

Mr Meta had been principal violinist of the Riganveldt Family Orchestra for almost 20 years when he was replaced and claimed not to mind. Of course this wasn't the whole truth – Meta did mind, very much, and it was to set in motion a quite unexpected chain of events.

For a long time the orchestra was nothing more than a well-meaning bunch of amateurs. There was no percussion section, and not a single cello. They had flutes but no piccolo. Violins but no viola. Clarinets they had to shrill excess. They rehearsed in the drill hall by the harbour – the salt air was corrosive but the town required an orchestra, so it was the duty of those with talent or instrument to attend on Mondays and Thursdays at 6pm sharp.

Then in the winter of '72 Meta was called to attend the conductor, Hebbel Flink. Flink spent his days driving either the V or VII tram, so this meant a morning of scuttling across town to catch him at the wheel. It was breathless work at Meta's time of life, which wasn't old exactly, but decidedly measured.

"What's this business?" It was February and Meta, wearing two jumpers inside his coat, was shivering.

"Ah, Meta!" Flink cried. Meta had been hovering beside the diver's cab for several stops, but Flink liked to express surprise at every given opportunity. "How's life?"

Flink jangled the cord and the tram moved off. Party members were stuffed in the back of the vehicle, briefcases pressed against their laps.

"Looks like I'll be late," Meta prompted.

"Not to worry old chap! I'll sign your chit, pass it here."

Meta slid his permit under the driver's window and asked again what the business was.

"Ah, you'll like this!" Flink declared.

It transpired that a Party member had recently moved to town. Flink didn't have all the details, but there was something about a conflict of interest, a cross-department transfer, and a Bechmann ebony violin (second hand). In short there was a new player, and Meta was to extend a welcome, copy the repertoire, arrange the seating and so forth. Meta bristled – not for the task, but for the asking of it: hadn't he been leader of the orchestra long enough to know what was expected of him?

However the request came about, Meta performed his role as was fitting. He spent the next few evenings copying out the orchestra's repertoire until his hand ached and his dreams danced along to quarter notes. Mrs Meta, who was full of sense in direct correlation to Meta's sense of propriety, watched all of this with almost divine patience.

Finally she queried: "But need it all be done at once?" They'd been married 40 years, and Mrs Meta said the secret was to always speak what was in the heart with honesty and impunity.

She propped her head on her hand and smiled.

"Perhaps this violinist fellow won't even stay."

Meta slid a pile of papers across the table. "You start on these. Don't forget the incidentals." After a moment's thought he added: "No need to add the hairpins." Volume, after all, was the conductor's privilege.

The new violinist, Alice Gerhad, turned out to be a decent player who took discounted lessons once a week. Perhaps it was the lessons, or perhaps it was her position in the Party, but within weeks Meta was riding the trams once more.

"Meta!" Flink cried. "Listen, I was thinking – of course, only with your express satisfaction with the affair – perhaps Ms Gerhad might benefit from leading for some time? Purely a trial run. Purely your say-so!"

But it wasn't his say-so, was it? Meta was an old-school musician: the conductor's word was law.

It was March and the snow was a foot high. The tram stalled on the corner of Herringsval and all were forced to alight. Flink was too busy to sign Meta's permit so he lost the morning's pay, but so it went.

Rehearsals continued through spring, cycling through Bach and Beethoven. Meta was nudged down a desk so that Gerhad could sit beside a woman, as was appropriate. Then both second violins – husband and wife – fell ill and Meta was shunted over to cover their parts. Meta didn't mind, but the work became drudgery. There was less melody, and more counting. He twisted his elbows to get up into the high positions but it wasn't his métier and the strangled notes of little reward. Why make a violin sound like a flute – weren't there flutes enough? There were already seven of them plus clarinets, and at times Meta felt he was understudy to a wind band.

"Wind band? Wind bag, more like!"

That was how he felt about it, though only Mrs Meta was party to the sentiment. What Mrs Meta made of it was not immediately clear, however; she was concentrating, because they were watching TV with the sound off.

They lived in a housing block, functional and fitted with the necessary comforts, but not built for privacy. The walls were thin and told everything, so they lived at low volume in deference to neighbours on the other side of the compound. No matter: it turned out telling their own stories alongside the muted television was far more satisfying.

"This man is a revolutionary," Mrs Meta said. "He and Carlo are planning something – just you watch!"

Meta hushed her with his hand. "Neighbours," he said. "Which one's Carlo again?"

"The one with the beard. Anyway, why not have a break from the orchestra?"

They were eating potatoes in chicken sauce without the chicken, because it was mid-week. Meta made an angry mash.

"On what grounds? Someone took my seat?"

"Why not? That would be entirely reasonable after all this time – surely they don't need it be spelled out? Do you? You haven't missed a rehearsal in almost 12 years. The Lord had a day off after a single week!"

"Well the Lord had no one to judge *him*. Besides ..."

Besides, demotion or not, Meta had retained responsibilities which, for one reason or another, weren't simply given to Gerhad. He went in early to lay out the seats, and stayed late to clear them away again. If Flink secured a score it was Meta's job to copy out the individual parts. And at least three times a month he crossed town on his own dime to ask some official or other if any function was planned, or to offer the services of the orchestra otherwise. It was useful work – you could call it important, even – but it was also tiring and thankless and seemingly never-ending.

Social duty was unavoidable, of course, but then the matter came to an unexpected and painful resolution: walking home across the park one evening, Meta was struck by a cricket ball. It flew out of the twilight sky like a bad-tempered bird and landed, excruciatingly, on his left elbow. This was both good and bad luck – he was right-handed, so it didn't stop his work or wages, but it was to incapacitate his violin playing for quite some time.

Meta took his elbow along to the following rehearsal, showing off the swelling to quite the to-do:

"Good grief!"

"We should see the the size of the other fellow, eh, Meta?"

And Meta's favourite line of inquiry, "What *have* you been doing to yourself?"

Then Flink said, "Doctors, eh! What did he tell you?" and Meta was stumped. It hadn't occurred to him to call on the doctor. People went to a doctor when they didn't know what was wrong with them, but he knew exactly what was wrong with him: he'd been hit by a cricket ball.

"Oh, ice. Keep it elevated." Then he added quickly, so as to remove any doubt: "And not move it much, you know – no playing for a while, I'm afraid!" It wasn't a lie as such; it was merely common sense.

A tiny woman with an incredible capacity for blowing the wrong notes peered up at him.

"Who did you see, Meta?"

"It wasn't that foreign doctor, was it?" someone else asked. "I never understand what he's saying. I don't think he does, either!"

"Actually I consulted my cousin," Meta announced, with the air of one unaccustomed to dealing out his private affairs like street-corner candies (true). "He's a doctor" (untrue: he gutted fish for a living. Meta walked home in a thin sweat).

Still, the lie came with a buffer; a thin margin in which Meta's time was his own. He bought a stack of detective novels and shivered at the easy violence. He found a Latin dictionary and memorised everything beginning with A. Mrs Meta tested him and he got top marks – but it was just a list of words without slots to put them in. He sketched a little, but his drawings were rudimentary.

"Well what does that matter?" Mrs Meta asked. Meta knew it *did* matter, but couldn't say why.

The violin was there through all of this, spruce and maple bound in the brace of a shared rib. He returned to it one evening and found it played well, honeyed and melodious – it was as if the violin played its own true nature and Meta were merely the conduit.

Still, Mrs Meta would listen from the living room with a smile. Meta was good – not great, but sweet enough – and those who knew him took delight in his playing. That was the miracle of the instrument: not that two halves could be so harmonious, but that they were ever other than one piece.

Meta started playing again regularly, 20 minutes at a time. Then his elbow would grow stiff, the pain flaring up into his shoulder, and he'd place the violin in its coffin and throw down the lid. Returning to the orchestra was out of the question, yet the guilt of it needled him badly. For one thing, just before the cricket ball incident, Meta had secured a performance: the Heichmann Academy 'passing out'. It was a coup, of a kind, and there was much organising to be done as a result – and no Meta to be doing it.

Meta rolled up his sleeve. The blackened bruise had grown through shades of purple and pale pink and there was no trace of it now. He could hardly take his elbow back to Flink in such pristine condition; it just didn't seem believable.

He fretted about it for a few days, then ripped an old baby blanket into strips and wound it around his arm. It was an untidy mess and he'd started too high up: he looked more dressed for mourning than for agony. Mrs Meta was furious:

"What a thing! What were you thinking? And how dare you?"

"It's not as if we'd need it again."

"That is not the point!" She slammed the bedroom door, then opened it almost immediately. "Why not just tell Flink you don't want to play? Why all this ridiculousness?"

Guilt was why. Meta couldn't play for more than 20 minutes at a time, that much was true. But his feeling about the matter, that was something else. Secretly, he was relieved.

Then Flink phoned to say he would call at the apartment, and Meta was gripped by fresh panic. He ran into the bedroom looking for the bandage, but the blanket had been reassembled with rough, looping stitches. He cursed and threw it under the bed, then put on two long-sleeved jumpers and a dressing gown and came out casually.

Flink arrived 20 minutes later, threw himself onto the sofa, and refused coffee, tea, spiced gin, and water. Whether he cocked an eyebrow at Meta's garb or the wallpaper was his own affair.

"Ah, Meta! Yes, we were just saying amongst ourselves – the orchestra, you know – that we missed you. It's a dreadful shame you won't be at the Heichmann. We've got so much planning to do now, so many things to sort out." He pulled a long face which conveyed the burden of things to be done.

"Still, you just think about getting better old man, never you mind about our woes! No, I came to show you this."

He unravelled a bundle of pages. It was a mock symphony, Flink's own construction, scratched out in pencil and passion. At the top he'd printed:

## *META VARIATIONS.*

Meta blinked several times and swallowed hard. The gesture was touching, though on investigation there was that familiar sense of discord among the notes: Flink had distilled the essence of the orchestra and laid it out on paper in its true bones. Meta read it over for some time, blushing between pride and embarrassment and back again.

"No rush, old man," Flink was saying. 'Don't get up!"

"What's no rush?" Meta asked, but Flink's coat was already brushing against the wall, and then the front door slammed. His footsteps echoed in the metal stairwell for some time, as if he was still out there and clambering up and down for a lark.

"What's no rush?" Meta asked the clock.

Mrs Meta, who appeared to have been listening from the kitchen, folded her arms. "Of all the things – he means you to copy out the parts. Can't someone else do _t? Can't he?"

"He works."

"Who doesn't!"

"And the others read only their own own parts, you know."

"Well, my God, then! It's just copying, isn't it?"

She peered at the sheets and sniffed.

"Looks derivative to me. Bach, Bruhbohn ... what a mess!"

Meta was surprised. "What do you know of Bruhbohn?"

"I have ears, don't I?"

He shook his head – not in disagreement, of course, but because this was how things were.

"He wrote it for me. It would be churlish not to help."

"He wrote your name on it," Mrs Meta pointed out.

Meta reached under the sofa for a pad of manuscript paper and licked the nib of his pen.

"What's for dinner?"

She tutted, but he could no longer hear her. He was poring over the notes spread before him, totting them up in his head like columns of numbers. Then he ripped off a sheet of lined paper and started to write. He caught the pulse, passed it from violin to horn, and returned it in the clarinet. He hummed the melody, and gave it to the flutes. He dropped it an octave and sliced it into running quavers scattered across the ledger lines. He muted the trills and added rests, and gave it space to breathe.

Night drew on, and across the compound the lights of a hundred apartments extinguished one by one. It was dark, and Mrs Meta had gone to bed, but the symphony was finished – and it was a fine thing.

Meta split the parts into their portions, wrapped each with a string, and slid them into an envelope. In the morning he dropped it off at the city's snarling transport hub, from where it would make its way to Flink.

There was a blank period of weeks after that in which life moved sluggish and dull. There was work six days a week in the cramped office on Berganville, with lunch taken on a bench in the park. Quiet evenings with the TV turned low. There were minor scales, laborious in their fingering and tones but with their own kind of downcast beauty. Spring evaporated by the side of the road. The sky grew to blue once more, and even strangers chanced a smile in passing.

Then one lunchtime there was a discarded copy of the Chronicle's evening edition. Next to the classifieds was a photograph of the Riganveldt Family Orchestra and an entire column of 10-point type: how the orchestra had premiered a new work at the Heichmann Academy and it had been an immediate and stirring success amongst audience and noted reviewers. The principal work had been composed by conductor Hebbel Flink *in memoriam* for one of the orchestra's own. A full review by Henrik Wahber was to follow. Meta read the column twice, swallowed hard, then tore it out and put it in his pocket.

He spent an hour after work circling on the VII, finally catching words with the young man in the driver's cab.

"Mr Flink?" The driver grinned. "He's gone to New York."

Meta fish-mouthed for a full minute.

"In America?"

"No, the one on the Russian Steppe. Of course in America. New York!"

"But why? When?"

"He sailed on Monday. He leads the orchestra. They've all gone."

"He conducts it," Meta corrected the young man. Then the subtlety struck him: "*All of them?*"

"Mr Flink composed a tune, and he was invited to perform it in New York. Our Mr Flink! Fancy that!" The driver pushed his cap up on his head and grinned as though Flink's good fortune was for them all.

Meta was less thrilled. All those years of service, and he wasn't invited, wasn't included, wasn't even informed. Then there was the question of the Meta Variations: did he or did he not have a significant role in that? Yet here he was uncredited and unknown. He was a silent partner and, worse than that, he feared he was no partner at all.

News came in half-chewed morsels. The orchestra was a success; Flink was a genius. It was an achievement which reflected on the whole town – "what is the orchestra, if not all of us?" the Chronicle opined. The orchestra performed in New York, then Washington. Kentucky and Boston. Canada. Germany. The Chronicle returned to more important affairs – economic growth, a cow on the highway – and the orchestra faded to a background hum. There was a final report placing them in Argentina, and then nothing.

Clocks slowed, and the weeks stretched on. Where were they? What had happened? Meta had vivid imaginings of a grand liner upended in the foamy Atlantic, manuscript papers floating on the waves. He imagined other scenarios, each more dramatic than the last – and then one evening he discovered Flink and co. were bone dry and in fine fettle. They were in full colour. They were on TV.

It was a Thursday. Meta had been watching a programme about milk production when, two hundred miles up, some satellite jumped in its orbit and yanked the TV's tuning knob a full four inches to the left. The dour-faced man talking with fervour about pump mechanics slid off screen. When the static cleared Meta was staring at a darkened auditorium. In the centre of the stage was the Riganveldt Family Orchestra.

They had grown – 10 desks of violins in two sections, a cone of cellists, a full row of brass – yet they were unmistakeable: there was Flink's milky pate under the spotlight.

Meta couldn't get his words out fast enough. "Turn it up!" he cried, "to hell with the neighbours!"

Velvet strings rolled around the living room chased by clarinets and flutes: breathless notes that crept into the curtain folds and burst like stars. It was the Meta Variations – *his* Meta Variations. The applause, when it came, was so loud that Meta was flattened in his chair. He stared open-mouthed at the TV – not at the spectacle of the orchestra or its new sound, but at the words in the corner of the screen:

*Symphony No. 4 (H. Flink)*
*Riganveldt City Orchestra (H. Flink).*

Meta turned it off. He stood by the set and gazed out of the window for some time. Then he turned to Mrs Meta and said, quite matter of factly, "Well. That's that."

Eventually the orchestra came home, though the first Meta knew of it was over breakfast some time later. The Chronicle had devoted an entire spread to their adventures, with illustrative map and notice of a gala concert featuring the world-famous Riganveldt City Orchestra at the end of the month.

Meta coughed explosively, brushed the coffee from his tie, folded his kipper into the newspaper, and placed the whole thing back on his plate. Then he went to see the Maestro.

Flink had moved up in the world: he'd been given an office overlooking the concrete Terminus. He looked up from his desk and blinked several times before smiling.

"Ah!" He got up to clasp Meta by the hand and elbow. "My old friend! It feels like a full year since I've seen you."

It had been 64 days.

"So tell me," Flink continued, "how are things, are you well?"

"Well, I'm not dead. That's something."

"That's always something!"

A bus honked somewhere below and then a second joined in as if to ring the hour in ugly duet.

"But you," Meta said, "you've had some adventures, I hear?"

"Meta, my man, it was wonderful! Such cities – such *size*. And the people we met, and who wanted to meet *us*. Ah, you should have been there –"

"How could I be there, Maestro? How could I be there, if I was dead?"

"Dead again, Meta?" Flink shook his head. "But this isn't healthy."

Meta brought out the newspaper clipping – by now thumbed quite black – and placed it on Flink's desk.

"First you tell the Chronicle that I'm dead. Then I'm dropped from the tour, just like that. And then the Meta Variations, which you say you wrote for me, well I'm dropped from that, too. It's insufferable!"

Flink scrutinised the clipping, looking from it to Meta several times in astonishment.

"Now look, old man … you've given all of this more weight than it deserves. Yes, you have – you've read a few things and taken the wrong view entirely. As it happens, I told a reporter I'd composed a symphony in benefit of a dear friend. If this is what he wrote, well, I had no part in it.

"As for renaming the symphony, that wasn't my intention. Believe me, I never suspected we – the Riganveldt City Orchestra! – would reach a global audience. But we did, and there are certain things which must happen as a result."

So there were reasons and digressions, and everything had its explanation.

Meta looked around the room. He wanted to say he'd written the symphony as much as Flink had, but it sounded a fiction built on jealousy. Events had conspired against him; the orchestra had been catapulted halfway around the world, and Meta had been kicked into line.

"You didn't even tell me you were going," he said instead.

Flink nodded. "Quite right. Yes, I deserve your anger on that score."

He sat back in his chair as though settling in for the blast.

Meta sighed. "No matter," he said nobly. "What additions to the repertoire? I expect I have some catching up to do."

"Ah," said Flink.

The orchestra had recruited several players along the way – solid, senior musicians. There was a Peruvian percussionist, an Armenian, and a flautist with several years of professional experience. Now there was a waiting list and an audition. They were no longer – with respect! – a half-formed bunch of troubadours. They were full. There was even talk of a junior orchestra composed of players from the region's schools to off-set the demand.

"Audition?"

Meta couldn't believe it. He still remembered the orchestra as it had existed before Flink; he'd composed the advertisement for a new conductor himself. Experience, when you laid it out and inspected it, was a blueprint: it showed you how things just were. But could it guide you to the new world? Not necessarily. It was a past tense business, not a map.

Flink, who was busy, turned back to his paperwork, and Meta left without saying goodbye. He walked home alongside a joyless procession of rush-hour traffic. He climbed the stairs slowly, entered the apartment, walked to the bedroom, and lay down dressed just as he was.

Mrs Meta tipped her head around the door. She noted the shoes on the bed. "What's all this?" she asked, but Meta turned over and wouldn't reply. He didn't say a word until the following morning when, still wrapped in his overcoat and outdoor shoes, he told her what had happened in Flink's office.

Mrs Meta swallowed a bolus of anger.

"Nonetheless, a grown man doesn't take to his bed over an injustice."

"What does he do?" Meta asked through the pillow.

"He fights it, inside and out. And he goes to work. And you'll be late."

"I'm not going," Meta said, and that was the end of the matter – except of course that it wasn't.

A note arrived a few days later advising Meta to report to the senior co-ordinator. Then there was a letter advising the householder to contact the senior co-ordinator or, failing that, to attend the Central Office of Employment with either medical note or death certificate (original, not copy).

"Ha," Meta scoffed. "Ask Flink – surely he has it."

Mrs Meta told him he was being ridiculous, but secretly she was concerned. The devil take the wages: she was worried about

Meta. He wouldn't eat, refused to leave the apartment, showed no interest in the TV, and barely spoke.

She turned up one lunchtime to find he'd papered the living room wall with orchestral scores. Her glorious wallpaper – mustard yellow with brown lozenge tessellation – was buried under a shiny veneer of sheet music. Meta had cooked up a glue from flour and water, and the whole apartment stank like the inside of a dumpling. When she asked him why, he just shrugged inside his overcoat.

Her first thought was to check on the violin, which at least was in one piece in its cardboard case. She stowed it away and wouldn't tell him where she'd put it.

"What is it to do with you?" Meta asked. "Can't I do what I like?"

Mrs Meta set her lips firmly. "Sometimes, no."

She was gone a long time and Meta, who had been numb for days, felt hunger return like a fresh wound. He sat in front of their wedding photo, agitating the frame back and forth on its shelf. They were smiling in the photo, as though they knew the rumour of fleeting moments and had no fear of it. Mrs Meta was wearing a flowery dress – maybe yellow, he was no longer sure – with a lace shawl pinned in her hair. He faced Mrs Meta in the picture and asked as though she could reply, "where have you gone?"

Eventually Mrs Meta returned with a halibut in a net bag, and the mail, which included a wide envelope containing a handwritten score. It was another Flink composition.

Meta ran the envelope across the seat of his pants.

"Why send it here? What do I care? I could find more genius than this in a used tissue."

"Flink asked for your help. So you can't rejoin the orchestra, so what? This way you can still be involved."

"I don't want to be involved with those charlatans!" Meta shouted. He'd grown quite flushed in his face. Mrs Meta took this as a good sign.

"I've been thinking," she said.

The second hand of the clock chased the first while she explained. Meta listened, shaking his head impatiently.

"That wouldn't work," he said at last, and told her why.

This went on for some time, their low voices brewing the same thought, stretching it out, picking it over. The fish on the counter grew slowly grey-faced: they were too busy to eat.

Mrs Meta boiled a pan of water and started on the living room wall. She soaked the glue until it softened, then scraped away fragments of the Riezler Suite, Dormer Tansey and On a Spring Afternoon. Meta unfolded Flink's latest symphony and copied each line to a fresh sheet of paper, grouping first flute and second flute, then first clarinet and second clarinet. After an hour they switched, one piling up fresh papers on the low table and the other stripping them back from the wall.

They tidied as they went, building up Flink's melody in places, paring it back in others. They sliced whole notes in half, and in half again, and polished a rumbling echo until it thundered magnificent beneath the exterior. Even Mrs Meta, who had never held an instrument, had over the years discerned what made them play and to what degree. Meta watched her with a rag in his hand and a deep sense of admiration.

By morning they'd finished a third of the symphony's parts, with the living room wall likewise a canvas of mess and bare plaster – but it was moving; it was on its way. Still, Meta turned glum at the thought of going back to work.

"Tell them your uncle died." Mrs Meta, gripped by the momentum of activity, thought and spoke quickly. "The one out in the sticks – tell them he died."

"But he died last year."

"Yes, and you never took leave of absence."

"But now it's a lie."

"Not really. Besides, it would take them months to check, and they'd give up within a week!"

She watched him frown, then linked her arm through his and held on.

"This is our small corner of the world. There's not much to it, but if we don't cling to what we have, the world would shake us off and keep turning."

So it was decided. Meta parcelled up the completed pages and dropped them off at the Terminus. He pushed them under Flink's door with a note informing that there were enough parts to cycle through the whole work, with the remainder to follow. Meta realised it was cutting things fine, but with other commitments and his elbow it was the best he could do. Rest assured, the remainder would come on time. Sincerely, etc. etc.

Every night that week there was a fast and simple supper: potatoes and chives one evening; a bowl of rice on another; thin soup; a plate of crackers. After they ate they pulled their chairs under the table and worked until late. The TV stayed off, blank-eyed and watchful; they went about their lives quietly, marking time on paper.

Finally, the symphony was ready. They read it over, each pointing out the lines they'd constructed, humming them under their breath. Mrs Meta fetched the violin from the back of the linen cupboard and Meta played passages on request, transposing as he went.

Mrs Meta threw open the windows and on and on he played until even the neighbours thumped the walls. Mrs Meta shouted "encore!", and they caught themselves laughing, giddy and creased in yesterday's clothes.

They took turns steeping in the tub. Meta dried his wife's hair with a towel and she laid out his suit. They dressed, helped each other into their coats, and slowly descended the stairs.

Summer hung above central district. That is, the trees in the park were still bare, but overhead the clouds came in thin streaks. Behind them trailed wide skirts of blue sky and, far off in the distance, the distinctive patterns of Tarlet gulls carried home on the jet stream.

Meta looked worried.

"I think we'll be late."

"We're early yet!"

"What I mean is, I think we'll be found out."

Mrs Meta stopped and turned her face to the evening sky. She closed her eyes as if to lay into memory this return to warmth. She seemed quite unperturbed when she told Meta, "Yes, I think we will. How could we not?"

They were walking across the bridge, measuring out their steps. The Zehn flowed on beneath them, green and viscous and in no particular rush to reach its end.

"We're putting everything on the line. Our reputation, our peace. And Flink will take the matter further, of course. Is it worth it for a petty revenge? No. We'll forget it and go home."

"We can't go home: Flink's waiting for the score. You can imagine the fuss if the orchestra can't start with half the town waiting! We're in it now, whatever you say."

She spoke calmly but Meta felt his resolve dropping away. Mrs Meta placed a hand on his arm.

"Sometimes," she said, "it's OK to make the wrong decision."

"In what possible way can you mean?"

"Well, how else do people like us leave a mark on the world? We work, we eat, we work, we pay taxes. We go without. We own nothing, but we have all the responsibilities of Party members."

Meta glanced around at this seditious thought, but there was no one in sight. There was just the river and the clouds and the slow climb towards the concert hall.

"I think it must be OK to take a gamble on mischief after all these years of making the best of not much at all."

Mrs Meta looked uncharacteristically sad a moment.

"So the world doesn't recognise talents like ours – do we just stop using them?"

Meta was shocked.

"Why, any petty criminal could say the same thing!"

"You know what I mean," Mrs Meta said. "Here we are, paying on the door to listen to the symphony you wrote. The world has called you a genius, yet you think yourself a mediocre man. If I didn't love you I could happily push you into the river."

It was growing dark and the temperature was dropping in half steps, but Meta was struck by how fresh the day still was. There was no traffic now, no smog to suffocate the senses. There were birds in Stollen Square singing nonsense. The world, when you stopped to consider it, was of no great construct.

He turned to Mrs Meta and smiled.

"Push me into the river? My dear, you could heave mountains into the sea if the feeling took you."

The concert hall was a fat, grey building with all the pomp of a medieval castle and none of its charm. Meta paid for tickets, left Mrs Meta at the lobby, and walked alone to the back entrance.

There was hoo-ha at the stage door, and then he was inside and scurrying through corridors lined with folded chairs, costumes and, somewhat alarmingly, 5 life-size prosthetic legs propped against a wall. This was the building's back passage – gilded up front but unseemly and somehow offensive at close quarters. Finally he turned left and there was Flink just coming out of a dressing room.

"My God, man – what were you thinking? Thanks to your delays we're barely rehearsed. I would have asked someone else if I'd known it was such a trouble!"

Meta, still clasping the envelope, blinked. "Why didn't you?" He wasn't being rude; it was just that the thought had never occurred to him before.

Flink wouldn't say. He grabbed the score and thumbed it as though he could transmit the intensity of his wrath through his fingers.

"So, everything is here. But damn it, you've put me in a terrible position. It won't do at all!"

Meta didn't know what else he could add to this, so bowed.

"Best of luck. We can't wait to hear the symphony. Break your leg!"

Flink shot him a look of disgust and closed the door gently but firmly in his face. From inside the room, Meta heard violins.

The Chronicle would later describe the concert as an odd affair, and no doubt it was that. The first movement was rapid and entrancing; there were two melodies, one light and laughing, the other a grim whisper. They coiled about each other and painted strange pictures in the darkened auditorium. They resonated, and the more sensitive members of the audience shivered and gripped themselves.

There was a brief, satisfied pause when the movement concluded. The members of the orchestra fussed with their music and fixed sombre expressions on their faces. Then Flink sank his shoulders in preparation, raised his hands, and brought the adagio into being.

The second movement was solemn and weighty, and slow enough that something which had lain hidden in the earlier piece crept from between the strings and the woodwind. The same encircled melodies were revisited in this piece, but now there was something disconcerting about them. One could strain the ears or shake one's head and commit to paying more attention, but it was intangible. It was like a jet plane at take-off, drowning the audible world in its hum, yet the dogged intuition that underneath the fury, someone was screaming.

The audience shifted and squirmed; some of them even broke out into whispers. The orchestra played on. Flink played on. He raised his hands and leaned in to the fight. Around his head lay a familiar tiara of sweat.

The third movement, when it came, was monstrous. Flink would later speculate that whole passages had been copied in maliciously – backwards, in rounds and shared across instruments so that one could never quite catch its tail. There were crimson notes laid alongside orange ones. The melody was repeated in a dropped octave and played at abominable pace, as if one tune was ever mimicking the other like a cruelty. *Hideous*, Henrik Wahber would write for the Chronicle: graceless and garish expressionism in its worst excess; this was Beethoven, had Beethoven been deaf and a masochist.

Whether this was fair judgement wasn't for Meta to say: he didn't hear the third movement performed that evening, and never would. As the adagio swelled to its close Mrs Meta had squeezed Meta's hand beneath their coats; that was their cue to leave.

Outside evening had come on. There was a suggestion of clouds overhead, but no certainty. They dawdled in the doorway as though there was no plan from this point.

"Well," Mrs Meta murmured, "what should we do now?"

Meta didn't know. He had two conflicting emotions just then. One was the kind of satisfaction that comes from a small but deserved victory. The other involved him sinking beneath the sludgy river while the clouds floated unseen overhead.

Mrs Meta was watching him with a lop-sided smile. The street lights had been dimmed and in the dark she looked unnervingly like her wedding photo. He took her arm.

"We'll go home via Grinksi Street. I heard there's a bar there serving home-made booze and an unspeakable cabaret in the back room. We'll go there; we'll get drunk. We'll order the whole menu between us, and then we'll climb out of the storeroom window before the bill comes. Of course you're wearing heels, but that can only help. I'll bend down like a bench, so you'll climb out first. Then we'll stagger home by moonlight, and I'll enact choice scenes from the rogue's cabaret."

"You seem very familiar with the logistics of this storeroom. This is some place you've only heard of, you say?"

"It was some place I dreamt."

"It sounds enchanting. We should go."

They shared a smile; the same smile.

"Perhaps another time," Meta said. "Let's go home."

They crossed the bridge in silence. Even the birds had stopped their music. Meta stood undecided for a moment.

"You go on ahead; I'll catch you up."

Mrs Meta regarded him carefully then walked on, her coat flapping slow applause. Meta stood on the bridge and watched the river. The water was dark, and the evening was dark, and there was no separation between the two. He looked down for the water and couldn't find it – sometimes, he supposed, such things were an act of faith.

He reached into his pocket and drew out Flink's manuscript. Handwritten in pencil and passion, it was the only copy of the original. Meta rolled it up, tapped it in the palm of his hand, and dropped it over the balustrade. Immediately it was gone, swallowed by the dark, or swallowed by the water – either way it was immaterial.

He caught Mrs Meta up at the corner, and they walked on slowly – not old, exactly, but decidedly measured.

"So, what's so unspeakable about this cabaret?" Mrs Meta wanted to know.

"There is no cabaret." He looked for her face and couldn't quite make it out in the dark.

"Tell me anyway," he heard her say.

So he did.

# *Escapology*

It was sometime between one dull war and the next. Excitement lay in everyday things: in box-cut coats and the revolution of Nylon – and then, one day, in a packing crate stuffed with straw and stinking of moth balls.

"Look!" Bobby screeched, lips stretched in a mauve smile. She wasn't the right side of 40 for the shade but it wasn't for Ray Bardon to say it; it was barely proper to think it.

Bobby rummaged through the crate, straw flying up and floating down over the silk-weave rug. Finally she straightened up, holding a hinged case of dense, dark wood.

"Look!" she cried again. "Isn't it darling?"

"Quite. What is it?"

"Oh, Ray! It's a Christmas calendar. It's an antique. It must be at least 50 years old! It's German."

"What the hell!" Curiosity won out. "A what?"

It was a mahogany box about two-foot square, with a rich, just-buffed gleam to it. The whole thing opened out like stage curtains to reveal a solid interior peppered with tiny doors. Bobby fiddled her nail under a catch and one jumped open, and then they both stood peering down at the miniature landscape which had slid into view.

"It's an Advent calendar." Bobby showed him the delicately stencilled dates. "One door for each day of the month until Christmas Eve. Oh, Ray, isn't it the most –"

"Darling thing, yes." It was the most redundant bauble Ray had ever seen. "Where'd you get it?"

"Bertram's."

"The dress maker?"

"Bertie was getting rid of it – he's been getting rid of lots of things. Did you hear his wife left?"

"Left my foot. You know what they're saying, don't you? I don't want you going there any more. Go to Delfini's. Hell, go buy your clothes off the rack like everyone else."

Bobby giggled. "Oh Ray, you make the funniest jokes."

"Yeah. Now you tell one. How much did this piece of darling cost me?"

She told him and, for a moment, the world turned white. Ray gripped the back of the armchair.

"Oh, Ray – are you ... you're not angry, are you? He was practically giving it away!"

She creased her face in the manner of a teenage coquette. Ray felt queasy watching her.

"You know what it is? A fella's just hungry. How about you get to work on those chops? I could eat the whole farm."

"Oh, Ray!"

She'd been so distracted by the fuss in the shop, then getting the calendar back to the apartment, and then the excitement at home, and it was only when the door had slammed and there was Ray standing there in his uniform ...

"Forget it." Ray picked up the newspaper and shook it out.

"Tuna salad?" She peeped over the headlines and worked her eyelashes in a mockery of seduction.

Ray felt a wave of sourness in his stomach.

"Anything. Open a can. Knock yourself out."


The Advent calendar squatted on the sideboard for a couple of weeks gathering dust and finger marks, and then it was

December. Star-like lights appeared on Oak Street, and department stores took to dressing their windows with nativity scenes and clockwork puppets.

Roberta was unbearable in winter: everything overjoyed her, from the prospect of a new wardrobe to the first dusting of snow. December was the worst. It was as if she went into a month-long sugary high, cooing and screeching carols at any given moment, as though Christmas Day came once a decade instead of as regularly as January or March.

Ray watched her festoon the apartment with garlands and trinkets. He dutifully tugged a dead tree up four flights of stairs and then, when Bobby was busy making some list or other, dressed it himself.

The wooden calendar played its role in all of this with seasoned aplomb, rosy and sleek under the electric lights. Each evening Bobby flew to the sideboard, ice clinking in her glass, a cigarette jammed into an ivory holder. Peeping behind the calendar's miniature doors – peering into miniature worlds – was worthy of ceremony. It was grand and exotic and, by association, so were they.

"Ready?" Bobby would cry, "ready?"

December 1: A lakeside country scene – snow drifts piled about like the hills of merry olde England and a skulk of foxes sleeping in the corner of the frame.

December 2: The frozen lake at night, stars strewn across a midnight canvas and one shining brighter than all the rest.

December 3: The solitary house on the far shore with its three stories and garret windows. Perfect, like a doll's house, with candles blazing in the ground floor windows and a procession of carriages in the drive.

December 4: The foxes awake, prancing in the snow and chasing their tails – a darling scene.

December 5: The most delicate pink slippers by the side of the lake, silk and embroidered with beads and –

"And what?" Ray threw down the newspaper. "Slippers by the lake. And?"

Bobby shook her head. "It's the oddest thing."

He went to stand beside her, holding his breath against the insult of camphor hitting perfume. There was the frozen lake, blue and glassy under the night sky, snow in the foreground like grey ticking. There was an interesting trick of perspective, as though they were perched among the branches and peeping down on a secret scene. The artist had painstakingly drawn two slippers by the side of the lake, silken and tangible in the moonlight. Under the ice, a little way from the bank, was a shadow.

"Well now … what do you think that is?"

Ray reached for his lighter. The flame danced then steadied, illuminating the lake and the shape of a woman fixed under the ice, pale as Ophelia, hair streaming behind her.

Ray gave a long whistle.

"Oh, don't look like that. It's an artist's pun. And you said it was German, right? Anyway, some starving artisan probably had to paint a hundred of these. You can't blame him for wanting to make a little mischief every now and then."

"It's an Advent calendar! What if a child opened the door?"

*Not at this price.* The thought of it turned his stomach.

"Well if you can't laugh about it, at least have a drink."

Bobby was crooning nervously to herself: Hark the Herald cranked up an octave.

"Turn the radio up," he snapped. "Can't hear a damn thing." He blocked the sight of her with his newspaper, and turned back to page 4.

The floating shadow under the lake was a minor sourness, after which the miniature scenes revisited darling, snow-filled vistas. A party of skaters appeared on the ice, frolicking in their mittens and sheer-bladed boots. Another day it was noon and the sun picked out holly hung over the door of the lake house; paw prints in the snow; a jetty on the far bank.

Then one evening Ray came home to find the radio playing boisterously and Bobby wan-faced, her cigarette idling in its holster.

"What's the matter?"

Uncertainty stuck somewhere between his windpipe and his winter scarf; he wondered whether Frank had called round.

Bobby gestured at the calendar.

December 8: Moonlight hung hard over the snow while, in one corner, the adorable foxes snarled and bared fangs over the remains of a bloodied doe.

Ray poured a drink. So the foxes were having an early Christmas feast. So what? Why get upset about the natural order of things?

The blood had stained the snow. Amid the soil and scarlet a half-buried hand was just visible; a delicate hand with slender fingers and a single, red-stoned ring.

Ray heaved up the calendar and turned it over. The back was immaculate, fine grained and gleaming. In a corner, the faded whorls of a signature: Henry R. Marston.

"Are you sure this thing's German?"

"What does it matter?"

He shrugged.

"No," Bobby said. "Nasty, dirty little thing. No wonder Bertram didn't want it."

"You know Bertram's gone?"

Ray slung his overcoat over the armchair and stood with his uniform steaming in the warm room.

"I heard he just packed up and went. Ran off to some Pacific island, if you like that." He shook his head. "Can't say I blame him. I'd like a bit of sun right now, I can tell you. He's a free man, I guess. Still – whole thing's odd, that's for sure."

He wandered over to Bobby and placed a hand on her shoulder. She was icy under his touch.

"Why get in a state about it? I'll get rid of the damn thing." If he could get back even half of what it had cost him it might go some way to keeping Frank off his back. He looked around the apartment, its luxury wrappings dull under the dim lights. Maybe women never thought about complications like finances or even, half the time, dinner.

"Say," he said, sharply, "stop fretting and go fix supper."

Bobby looked up in surprise. She got up without a word and walked to the kitchen, pressing herself along the sides of the room as she went. Ray shook his head in wonder. If a bit of unease was all it took to make a woman more amenable, perhaps it had its upside. He thought about the kinds of men – brutes, really – who took to punishing their wives with affairs and mean words and fists. He mused on it for some time, and felt quite sick of the world.


Bobby didn't want to get rid of the calendar.

"It's an antique. And it's European."

She wanted to own it, yet she didn't care for it – and she certainly got little enjoyment from it. She kept it on the sideboard next to their souvenirs and the photo of Ray's brother, and insisted they open one door every evening.

"It's Christmas, Ray," she said reproachfully, as though the season were his fault.

Ray found himself caught between extremes of feeling. On the one hand the ambivlance of this latest purchase had stemmed Bobby's craving for ugly furniture. On the other, Frank still wanted what he was owed.

After a month of avoiding the guy, Frank had cornered him before the end of a late shift, materialising abruptly from behind the dockyard railings. It was raining, and with his hat down low Ray didn't know he was there until he was growling in his ear: "Bardon. How's tricks?"

Ray nodded, eyes on the desolate yard lying between him and the ocean. There was nothing to steal but scraps and iron filings: it was the promise of getting rich on pennies a day, stretched out over a decade or more. Who'd bother?

"Smoke, Frank?"

"You know, I'd rather have what you owe me."

"Sure. Listen, I already told you –"

"So you did, so you did. But that was last month and here I am still waiting. It wouldn't be so bad, Bardon, but I loaned you the money in good faith considering you were already in arrears. What gives, Ray? I mean, I ask myself: what does a man do with that much capital, and still coming to work in busted shoes. Hmm?"

He made a slow show of stretching his knuckles.

"Or you got a second family? You wouldn't be the first. Man gets tempted. Families are expensive. Heck, women are expensive. Rebecca spends it faster than you can make it, right?"

"Roberta," Ray said automatically, then punched himself through his pocket.

A whistle sounded in the distance, stifled by smog and the dirty night. Frank arranged his coat and pushed something into Ray's hand: it was a damp twenty.

"You think I'd begrudge you? What difference does it make now? Take it. You'll need it." He laughed, and his teeth rattled in his wide mouth.

It was gone ten by the time Ray got home. The radio was off and the whole place was hushed and sorry. He sniffed as he went in. It would be nice to come in from the cold just once to smell beef roasting in a pan, or mashed potatoes swimming in cream.

Bobby was waiting in a grey silk gown cut high on the neck and so low on the ankle so that it flowed around her as she sat. She looked tired and Ray realised she had stopped making up her face quite so garishly. He gave a start.

"Is that a new dress?"

She looked up in surprise. "No, not really."

"What do you mean, 'not really'? Is it new or not?"

"I mean it's not brand new." Brand a-new, she said, brand a-new, hanging onto the 'd' as though it were a precious gem. "I bought it a few weeks ago. You were there, remember?"

"No, I don't remember. Remind me."

"Why are you being like this? You're being ridiculous."

She rose, stately and offended, then stumbled over the hem of the gown and collapsed on him. They both fell against the wall, his arm lodged against her chest. She stared at him, her mouth stretched tight but the skin on her neck flapping loosely.

"I'm not an idiot! Don't take me for an idiot!"

"Oh, Ray – I don't! I never – I mean, I went. We." Gibberish. Panic. Gin on her breath.

He stared at her face and suddenly she looked so *old*. Was that how he looked? He flexed impressively against her clavicle, then felt a rush of shame. Here he was taking things out on her because she'd done nothing but take for twenty years while he'd shut his mouth and let her. He should confess. Now was the time to come clean. He tried to, and then her sing-song whine rang out:

"Don't you remember? You bought it for me. We bought it together. You said I should buy a ready-made dress. I didn't even want it!"

Ray backed away scraping his hands across his scalp.

"I remember." He glanced at her from under his lashes. "I'm sorry."

Bobby watched him warily, wordlessly.

"Listen, I'm a dull-headed idiot. You know that. You always had the elegance for the both of us. Don't hold it against me, will you? Listen. I want to give you your present early."

Ray ran into his bedroom and pulled the box out from the back of the closet. He came back and watched her tug away the satin bow.

"What's the matter? Don't you like it?"

Bobby lifted out the fox fur with a strange look on her face. It was a petite, caramel-coloured animal with glass eyes. There was a pin fixed to the jaw so that you could clamp the tail and it would look like it was holding it in its mouth.

"Like a scarf," he added redundantly.

Bobby's eyes flickered toward the sideboard, mouth turned down in a frown. Ray's hands itched terribly.

"You can't be serious? Look. Look at this thing!" He grabbed the fur out of her hands and flung it around his neck. "Why, it's *darling*, darling. You're not going to be influenced by a doll's house piece of crap, are you? Are you?"

He grabbed her and the two of them waltzed across the room to the waiting calendar.

"Go on. Open it. Let's see what tonight's seasonal cheer is, shall we?"

December 12: Twilight. Snow on the ground and whirling in the air. A woman was standing alone by the side of the lake. She was wearing a long grey gown; it and the lake were the same frosted shade. The woman had a strangely placid look on her face, and she was the spit of Mrs Bardon.

Bobby launched herself at the fireplace and stood sobbing over the mantelpiece. Ray stared at her, and then once more at her double in the calendar. Then he burst out laughing.

"Now that is a neat trick. Say, what is it you do with yourself all day? Taken up painting?"

He laughed for a long time and then, still shaking his head, left her to her tears and went out for dinner.

In between the crying jags, the nightly ritual continued. Gin waiting on the table. Bobby in her armchair.

December 14: The lake house. Solitary candle burning in an upstairs window; a woman in silhouette reading, perhaps, or sewing. Down in the driveway a man in a robe-like overcoat peered out at them from the shadows. He pressed a finger to his lips. The other hand, held loosely by his side, held a knife.

Bobby woke screaming that night. Ray ran to her room and found her trapped in the sheets, the mangled fox fur around her neck. He peeled it off and wiped her face with its tail.

"Why the heck did you wear it to bed?"

Her skin was papery under its night-cream mask, jowls wobbling in time to her trembling. She made a barnyard noise, eyes pulled wide and hair spreading around her like a root vegetable.

"Oh, Ray," she moaned, "I didn't."

She was half asleep, he realised, and he pinched her arm until she cried out.

"Then how come it's half strangling you, huh? You'll be telling me next that I put it on you!"

She wept, hands reaching out for him but he wanted none of it. He pushed her away and she fell against the pillows and sobbed like a movie star.

Bobby was pale and unkempt in the morning, with green shadows bedded in under her eyes. There was a great stripe around her neck, too, all mottled and marbled.

"They're some love bites you got there," Ray said. "Should I be jealous? Or should I just cut your nails?"

He stuffed the fox fur into its box and snapped the lid on.

"Don't plan on going out, Mrs Bardon. Last thing I need is the neighbours jumping to conclusions."

He considered asking a doctor to check in on her, and then he was struggling to fix the ribbon on the box and the thought evaporated.

On the way back from the store he stopped for a whiskey and a beef sandwich, and got hold of Frank. It was the combination of all three that had him feeling giddy, sliding around in thin slush and not minding the drizzle in his face. He skipped up the stairs and permitted himself a small dance on the third-floor landing.

He was still cheerful when he came into the apartment, but his eyebrows had crept up on his forehead. He shook the gift box that had been waiting outside the door.

"Silly old thing," he grinned, but Bobby looked away.

Inside the box was a pair of black brogues, real smart and shined to a high gloss. Ray whistled.

"And there's me having taken your present back. Boy, but we're some pair!"

Bobby opened her mouth, closed it, and shrugged. She had nothing much to say that day, or the next. Perhaps it was the silent treatment or perhaps, thought Ray, she was all talked out. Maybe they both were. You look at somebody's face every day for twenty years and finally there's nothing to see but wrinkles and dust.

Bobby packed her brown travelling case. It waited by the telephone table while the two of them staked out the apartment in silence and fumes.

December 17: Deserted lake. Snow on the trees, blood on the ice and not a soul to be seen.

December 18: Bobby opened the calendar and screamed at the devilish face pressed up against the frame as though it were rearing out at her. Ray snapped it shut.

"Why keep opening the damn thing if that's how you're going to carry on? What do you expect to see in there by now? Cherubs and chocolate boxes?"

"Don't you know why? Can't you see? That woman in there is me! That's me! How? How could it be?"

"You self-obsessed little harpy! And I suppose that leathery-faced ghoul in there is me, is it? You're a mean drunk, Roberta."

"You're a fine one to talk. You see it as plain as I do but you won't admit it. I wonder why that is?"

She tried to turn away but he caught her by the shoulders.

"Who asked you to spend my money on that ostentatious piece of crap? Did you ask me? Have you ever asked me about anything? No. You get some idea in your head and you go right ahead with it, and screw the consequences. And screw me, right? Spit on me. Rubbish me. Ridicule me. Well, if that's how you feel about it, go stay with your damn sister."

But Mrs Bardon couldn't leave, at least not straight away. It snowed so heavily that night that, come morning, the train station had vanished and there was a lumpen cloak of frosting in its place.

The Bardons sat in silence, ice glinting in their tumblers, waiting out that evening's dread. Radio playing softly in the background: static flares and big band. Ray toasted Mrs Bardon, then flicked a catch and peeped into the calendar.

Midnight, and all the stars in heaven looking on. A small fire on the lakeside, rosy and warming; cups of chocolate steaming on sticks. The party of skaters spun on the ice, holding hands and twirling in one great circle, smiles on their blushing faces.

They were skating around something lying on the ice: a woman in a neat travelling suit, the cape of the garment flung over her head and shoulders. A vanity case lay open to one side, flaunting its silk scarlet lining. No. Not scarlet. Bloodied. In the middle of the puckered fabric was the woman's head, upside down, neck sprouting like a champagne fountain. The red curve of her throat seeped like an inverted smile, or the puzzle of a frown. And then Ray saw, in the trees, a dark figure watching him: the man in the overcoat. He had his finger to his lips but there was no doubting it. He was grinning.

"Well?" Bobby asked from across the room.

Ray pressed the door shut.

"Foxes. Mating, rather vividly. You should take a look – it's quite some education!"

Bobby shook her head. Ray perched opposite her with a fresh glass.

"Cheer up, old bean."

She gave him a distant smile.

"You know what I think? A break would do you the world of good. Have a rest. Take in some country air. Catch up with your sister. Things will seem different after that. A new year, a new start. What d'you say?"

"I'd like that."

"Of course. Me too."

He stood up.

"They say the buses will be running tomorrow. I think I'll go down and get you that ticket. Then it's all taken care of and we can look forward to a new start."

"OK."

"OK then."

He pulled on his coat and carefully buffed a shoe against his trouser leg.

"Listen, Bobby. I've been honest with you about the pickle we got into. I shouldn't have kept it from you for so long and I'm sorry I did. But now you know. I'm going to fix it, but it's going to take some hard work. And sacrifice."

She nodded miserably as he reached out to her. She put her hand in his and he let her keep it there, feeling her skin against his. Then he slid off her ring and threw it into his pocket.

"I'm sorry, Bobby. If there was any other way you know I'd take it. But you've got to be reasonable: I can't keep magicking money out of thin air. You wait here. Relax. Enjoy yourself! I'll be home after the late shift, so don't wait up."

"I won't," she muttered – and she was true to her word.

By the time he came home Roberta had gone to bed, her door shut tight. Ray turned the radio on and let it play softly: strings racing trumpets, applause, cheers.

He went to the kitchen and unwrapped the sandwich he'd bought. He ran the faucet and sluiced water round the bottom of the gin bottle. He sliced a couple of lemons and then, with the band leader urging everyone to be upstanding in the other room, cut clean through the tip of his thumb.

"Goddamn you little –" he jammed his thumb in his mouth and threw the bloodied sandwich in the bin. Then, with nothing else to be had, he went back into the living room. He raised the bottle at the radio.

"God bless us, everyone!"

He slept in the armchair and when he woke the station had fizzled out into a blast of static. He roused himself and then dropped the bottle in fright.

His trousers were soaked in blood and for a moment he was gripped with numb terror for himself. The dull throbbing of his thumb cut through the fear and he realised he was still holding the knife in his other hand. Who knew a guy could bleed that much from just one finger?

He felt strung out. The lights in the room were dancing. He closed his eyes and the black behind them turned in waves. The radio hummed and shushed away. Roberta's door was still closed – and probably barricaded on the other side, he realised.

He got up and circled the room, the armchairs weaving around him. He gripped the front door as he passed and gave the little suitcase a smart kick. He looked at himself in the mirror. Pasty and bleary-eyed: quite some specimen.

He stooped over the wooden calendar, gave it a barber-shop knock, then fiddled with one of the tiny doors. He couldn't quite grasp the catch, gave a grunt, then finally caught it with his nail and flung it open.

There was no snow scene. There was no lake. There was a small room – it looked like a library or a den; wood panelling on the walls and shelves stuffed with leather-bound books. An illuminated globe in one corner. A bottle of port on the table. And in the middle of the room, looking out at him, a handsome chap in a dinner suit, legs stretched out on the table and a pipe in one hand. He looked the model of contentment. Yes, he looked the model of contentment.

Ray staggered on his feet and found himself leaning into the picture to give it a wink. And then, for some reason unknown, he plunged the knife into it. He sawed away, and then the little library was in the palm of his hand. He stroked it with his bloodied thumb, and stowed it in his pocket.

In the morning, Bobby was gone. Her bed was made, covers and corners folded neatly. Her suitcase was by the door where she'd left it, her coat was in the hall closet. Her hat, purse, gloves, cigarettes – all where they should be.

Ray pulled a coat over his pyjamas and stumbled downstairs. He threw open the front door and was momentarily blinded by the pristine snow. He waded ankle-deep to the back of the building and stood gazing up at Bobby's window.

Weintrauber, who lived on the second floor, gave him a pitying look. "Lost her, have you?"

Ray gave a smile in the corner of his mouth, and then his words fell out hoarsely:

"We had a stupid argument. I bought her a bus ticket yesterday and –" his hand flew to his coat pocket. "I guess she used it. I don't get women."

"Who does, Bardon; who does! Don't worry, old man – she'll be back. A smart woman knows she needs to make a man suffer. Else how do we learn? Eh?"

Ray thought about calling Bobby's sister, but when he picked up the receiver the phone spat and hissed angrily. Outside in the street the wires were bowed under snow garlands. Everything was at a standstill.

He waited for her to send word somehow, and then realised she wouldn't. Bobby went in for the dramatic. She'd probably turn up on New Year's Eve in a new dress, stinking of vermouth and recrimination. But why did she leave without her suitcase? Or her coat? A body would surely freeze without one. He shuddered. Should he phone the police or check the hospitals? He stopped himself. Bad news didn't wait for telephone wires.

He got cleaned up, then turned his attention to the apartment. He started by wiping down the worst of the dust. It was a good start and he found himself immersed in the task.

An hour later he'd rearranged the furniture and moved the clutter to one side of the room. When he surveyed the pile it was mammoth and impressive and enough to pay Frank back ten times over – and under his nose the whole time.

After a week he was over the worst of it. He'd been sick with worry, he'd been broken up – but if Bobby wanted to be Mrs Bardon then all in good time; they could discuss it.

Christmas came and went. He ate sandwiches for supper, and sometimes cooked, carefully timing a roast or pushing leftovers into a pot and leaving them to stew. He walked in the evenings, scuffing through the sleet, peeping at stars and lit windows. He drank beer, played a hand of cards, didn't begrudge his losings; stumbled back into the night with warm voices calling after him and a friendly hand on his back setting him right, sending him off.

Bobby didn't deign to call. He started clearing out her junk and uglies – decorative boxes, a hostess trolley, a jewelled telephone dialler – carrying them to a broker a few streets over. Some he off-loaded to the guys at work for pennies, and the endeavour turned out to be cathartic.

It got him looking for Frank, too, eventually locating him in a diner near the dockyard It was night, as it always seemed to be in December; fingers of ice curled round the doors and in every gasp of wind. Ray slid behind the table with an unexpected belch: "Say, Frank!"

"Bardon." Frank was busy with the gristle on a burger.

Ray slid an envelope across the table. A blurred fellow wearing a halo and a disconcerting grin mimicked him in the window.

"Just came to give you season's greetings, Frank."

Frank shot him a look.

"What's with the surprise?" Ray crowed, "you were planning to come visit me in hospital?"

Frank stroked the envelope with his thumb, glanced inside and slid it back across the table.

"What's the matter with you, Bardon? So you paid me. Big deal. Now you think you're the boss, pushing your money in my face? Take yourself off some place else. Ain't your wife waiting up for you?"

Frank was a big man made more impressive by the purple bruises fading on his chin, but he was surely mistaken. Ray watched him work the burger around his molars. After a while he pocketed the envelope and left without a word.

The snow fell fresh and untainted, taking back cars and lamp posts. Ray walked home slowly, watching the world unmake itself, and everything unknown.


New Year's night: a warm plate balanced on his knee, whiskey on the table. Waves of comfort and ease; tender meat, strong booze, a cigarette burning down in the ashtray.

Bobby's suitcase was still there, haughty by the door. Ray set his plate down and carried the case into the bedroom and shoved it away out of sight under the bed. Then he pulled it out and stood looking down at the deep leather creases. He knelt with his thumbs resting against the locks.

He hesitated and pushed the suitcase deep into the recess and, almost immediately, pulled it out again. Then, like a clock winding back, he took it to the front door and set it in its place. He felt his face burn. No. No man deserved to sit around and wait for Bobby Bardon to waltz back in. First thing. First thing in the morning he'd take it down to the dock and sink the damn thing.

The window was crested with snow, the night black beyond it. He fetched his coat from the closet and shrugged it on. He travelled around the room, swinging the hem across chairs and the bare telephone table. He let his thoughts ramble their own way. Life goes on. Fish in the sea, dead dogs: clichés, comforts, odd sayings.

His eyes lit on the wooden calendar and he found himself wondering why he'd kept it. It belonged to Bobby. It was her doing; her excessiveness. It had nearly ruined him, once. He draped the edge of his coat over it, sizing it up against the lining. He could carry it down along with the suitcase, why not? Yes. He would do it, and that would be the end of it.

He bent down to pick it up and saw that one door remained closed. December 24 held within it a tight-lipped mystery.

His hand went to his pocket and pulled out scraps of paper, crumpled notes, calculations – and the little scene from the library.

The handsome man smiled out from his den, pipe clouding away and the mirror behind him catching the candlelight and throwing it back into the room like beads, like pearls.

Ray crumpled the image between his fingers. The artist was no Rembrandt. His hand reached again for Christmas Eve, but at he last moment he lifted the whole calendar into his arms and cradled it against his chest. He carried it to the door and stooped to pick up the suitcase.

Things would be better in the new year, he thought. He'd be a different person. Life would be different; it might be possible even to be content.

He nodded at the memory of things which had once signified a shared existence: cut-crystal decanters, spilled tobacco, wax fruit, paper swans.

"Here's to you, Mrs Bardon," he said, and his voice rang hollow against the armchairs and the place where a rug had once lain.

He pulled his hat down low and departed, and the apartment went on without him: dark in its shadows, watchful for his return.

# The Gift

**January 9, 1999**

Rahul phoned in the early hours – just shy of 2am, when decent folk are asleep, or faking it until sun-up.

"Get round here." His voice was tinny at the end of the line. "There's something I have to show you. Something you need to see."

Gloomy intent lingered after I hung up. There was no emergency as far as I could tell; no life hanging in the balance. There was only curiosity, and that sense of foreboding that the dead hours bring. Of course I went.

Their house was dark, with just a blade of light peeking through an upstairs curtain. Rahul was standing at the door in a jumper and jeans – they looked slept in, but his face was lined for lack of rest. Behind him the living room had been marshalled into columns of boxes and packing crates. He gave me a glassy stare, the kind you find at the bottom of a bottle.

"Come upstairs."

He looked through me as he said it; through my coat and bones and into the street. I tried to laugh off the unease.

"I'm not that kind of girl!"

Rahul swayed to some unheard tune. I hadn't seen him more than twice in the last couple of months and he'd grown hollow, as though his insides had been misplaced while I wasn't looking.

We climbed the stairs in silence. There were bundles of letters to step over, fraying books, old cassettes, and a row of framed photos stacked on the landing. The photos were all of Claire of course, and that was no surprise, but this – this altar of her taking root while the rest of the house took flight – was unsettling and sad. She'd been dead four months.

I'd known Claire since university, Rahul too. Our histories twisted together going back years, but now there seemed nothing familiar about my memories of them or their home. The bedroom was inscrutable, with blind, browning shapes where frames and furniture had once rested. The bed was still there, but draped in greying sheets as though it too were dressed for departure.

Rahul gestured at a door in the corner of the room; they called it a walk-in closet, but it was nothing so grand as an airing cupboard.

"It's in there."

The closet door was ajar. Lamplight spread as far as the sill, only to be swallowed by the black on the other side. Curiosity fled.

"And what is it you've got in there?"

He gave me a long, empty look.

"You've known me forever," he said.

"American Lit. 106. You were in the wrong room."

"You've known me better than anyone. Almost anyone."

The house was silent. The world and its people were packed away in other rooms in other streets.

"What's going on, Rahul?"

"I just want you to remember that you know me, that's all."

"I know you. Got it." I gave a thumbs up, heart hammering in my throat.

Rahul stepped into the closet and disappeared from view. I thought about running downstairs and out of the house and away. The bed sheet wrinkled under my fingers, rough and unwashed, and I felt ashamed of myself. I didn't leave, and then the moment passed and it was too late.

Rahul came out of the closet backwards dragging a glass bottle. It was an enormous, old fashioned thing – green, with an almost perfectly round belly, and a thin neck rising as high as his knee. Something tumbled unevenly behind the mottled glass.

He dropped the bottle between us and the contents shivered and came to rest. Squinting down the neck I could see what they were: squares of paper – hundreds of them jumbled together like sugar clumps.

Rahul sat on the bed beside me, more paper squares scrunched in his fist.

"I want you to remember that you know me, and you knew Claire. We're normal people. We were. Still am. You remember?"

He placed a scrap of paper in my hand. It contained a single sentence in a blue familiar scrawl:

*June 15, 1996: Rahul and I get married.*

I read it twice, a thin bubble of nerves tickling the back of my throat.

"I don't follow."

Rahul turned it over. The back was a map of creases where it had once been folded and sealed with a strip of tape. Across the ripped tape was the remnant of a signature and another date, 27/10/1989.

He flipped the note to show me front and back, front and back, quickly like a semaphore.

"Do you see?"

I watched his face, his brown eyes beautiful above sunken cheeks and stubble.

"Claire and I were married on June 15th, 1996."

"Yes ..."

He pointed at the date on the back. "Claire wrote this the week we met, long before we were even dating. You were there – you know how long it took to get together. But Claire knew the date of our marriage before she even knew there was an us."

He told me this with buttoned-down excitement, as though he'd stumbled on some existential mystery, or Jesus' face on a bit of burnt toast.

"What are you saying – she manipulated you into marrying her?"

Rahul's body convulsed under the jumper. The laugh teetered on the brink of hysteria.

"I'm saying she predicted we'd get married, right down to the date."

I didn't realise I'd turned away, but found myself looking at the bedroom door. I summed the distance to the living room and timed the drive home.

"This seems significant to you; I get that." I spoke carefully, softly. "But Claire could have written this at any time."

"Good. Yes, she could have written it any time."

"So we shouldn't jump to any conclusions. Should we?"

Rahul nodded. He rubbed his hands as though settling in for a discussion about Proust or Pasternak.

"That's my signature," he admitted. "I signed it. I dated it. So I know for a fact that Claire wrote this 6 years before we'd set a wedding date."

"*You* signed it?" I glanced for the clock, but the table was gone and the time with it. "It's, what, 3 in the morning. You asked me to come, and I came, but enough with the bullshit."

He put his hand on my arm gently, as though I were the fragile one.

"Please – I'm trying to explain. Listen."

And so, incredulous, I listened.

All those years that Rahul had known Claire – while dating on-and-off at university, when they were shacked up together and, later, after they were married – she'd presented him periodically with a single slip of paper. Each time the paper was folded and sealed, its insides unknown. Claire would ask him to sign and date each one, on promise that he'd never read it, or any of the others. Rahul knew she where kept them, of course: at first there was a shoe box, and then a couple of carrier bags. Finally the paper scraps came to rest in the glass jar, where they bedded-in and multiplied. And yet, in al. that time, Rahul kept his word. Even after her death, and until a couple of days ago, he'd never pried.

"Just like that? Someone makes you sign a hundred pieces of paper over a decade and you never once think to ask what might be inside?"

"At first it was cute. Then it was a nothing favour. You know? It cost me nothing, and she asked me – serious, in earnest – and it cost me nothing to make her happy.

"I never had any doubts it would be anything harmful, anything other than good. Claire was that kind of person. That's what intimacy is, isn't it?"

"Well, that's beautiful," I said. "There you were so trusting, and there was Claire so trusting. How lovely."

We looked away into opposite corners of the room.

"God knows, I don't have your pain but I have a sense of it. You'd like to think Claire left some message for you, and here you have a hundred of them. But this isn't a prediction, it's a lucky guess. Or worse, it's a con trick. 'January 10th, 1999: I get mugged.' Well, then tomorrow I go hang around dark alleys. You see, don't you?"

"Human agency. Wish fulfilment. I get it."

He was nodding, placating, but there was something else, something as insistent as the room's musty odour. Rahul tapped the bottle with the side of his foot.

"You've only seen one. There are all the others."

He was still clutching a handful of notes; now he lay them in a row on the bed. There were different kinds of paper, each yellowing with age to a different degree. Two were scrawled in ink, one in pencil, but each followed the same template: a long form date and a 'prediction' on one side, and Rahul's date and signature on the other.

One signed in '93 gave the address of the house they would buy two years later. Another, dated months before we'd graduated contained a column of initials and exam marks – Claire's, Rahul's, even mine. It was a curious thing to see my initials scratched next to theirs.

"What about that one?"

I nodded at the one Rahul kept back. He held onto it tightly.

"Claire was pregnant."

I hadn't known about that – I hadn't known about any of it – and had the queerest feeling I was some place I shouldn't be.

A thought erased the emotion. What if the papers Claire had Rahul sign were blank? It's easy to predict things that are already a done deal. How would Rahul know? He'd never looked, he was too trusting – he'd said it himself and, for all his failings, I knew it was true of him. He was shot through with a seam of kindness; he wasn't a bad man, just sometimes childish.

I jammed a finger in the bottle and yanked out a paper. It was an inch long, and sealed with a strip of tape that snaked around it twice. The tape in turn was crossed by Rahul's signature, the thin whorls looping along both edges – it was unsophisticated and juvenile, but crudely tamper-proof. I ripped it open.

Outside the note was dated 14/3/1990. Inside Claire had written *August 27, 1991: Rahul breaks his promise. I forgive him.*

"What is it? What does it say?"

I held the note away from him, then ripped it into confetti and fed each piece into the neck of the bottle. He grabbed my hand and twisted it like he wanted to snap it clean off.

"What the hell are you doing?" His face, for the first time that night, wore something like real emotion.

"Trust me," I said, though I didn't know why I'd ripped it up. I didn't even know what I'd say to convince him otherwise.

"When did you break your promise?"

Rahul looked startled then guilty in quick succession.

"What promise?"

"Didn't you promise you wouldn't read Claire's notes?"

"Oh. Wednesday. Wednesday morning."

Relief came first, followed by thin chill and doubt.

"Is that what it said?" he asked. "You should have shown me. It wasn't yours to destroy!"

"Sorry. I wasn't thinking straight. Are you sure it was Wednesday?"

A car alarm firing up in the next street shocked the silence out of the room.

Rahul frowned.

"It wasn't long after we'd met. I thought it was a cute habit and it was, but of course I was curious. I wanted to know. So I opened one – just one."

"And? What did it bloody say?"

"*No cheating.*" He laughed and, for a fleeting moment, was boyish. "That was the only time."

"But she called you Rahul," I said. "In the notes. She called you Rahul."

"What do you think she called me – Mr Peiron?"

The car alarm climbed up and down in nonsense scales. I shut my eyes, blocking out the sight of Rahul and the hopeless room. I listened past the wailing car to the sound of my footsteps on the 2am pavement. I saw Rahul opening the front door, and ran my gaze in turn across each tower of boxes stacked in the living room.

I blinked, then looked from Rahul to the notes arranged on the bed sheet.

"She writes about you in the third person. In all of these notes – she wrote about you in the third person."

"So? So?"

He gripped my arm.

"I don't know! But she left the notes for you to find. Wasn't she writing them to you?"

It was awful to see the look on his face just then. The workings of his mind were played out in slow, painful motion as he retraced every step and doubt of the last two days.

"*Two days?*"

The thought came out of my mouth before I even knew I'd formed it. Rahul said he'd opened the first note two days ago, yet in that time he'd read a paltry handful. Instead he'd been sitting in the dark doing God knows what, and had only thought to call me a matter of hours ago.

I walked to the window and jerked it open through the curtain. The sudden wind was like steel to the innards. Outside the black sky had flushed orange; street lights braced for the coming dawn.

I knew what Rahul had been doing for two days. He'd been brewing dread and guilt, and now he wanted to share it with me. The bed creaked drily.

"What do you think?" His voice floated ghostly across the room. "Is there a note in there about us?"

94

"No. You're saying Claire had some kind of second sight – fine. I can see why you might think that. But Christ, there's a leap from that to omniscience.

"And anyway, if she knew, she'd have said something. She'd have done something."

"Would she? She knew she'd have a miscarriage but she still let herself go through it."

He dropped his head into his hands, battling the torrent of thought.

"We don't know what she thought. She never told you; not when it mattered."

It was a cheap shot, mitigated by truth.

"Why would someone write down all these things – things they knew would happen, and never do a thing about them? Why would she leave them for you to find?"

I have a theory, that the future is just a word for all the things that happen to you. The future happens however you feel about it; it's a juggernaut that can't be derailed by tears or prayers or hard work.

Second sight, if such a thing exists, is a sickness; a proper Greek tragedy of a punishment. If Claire had it she must have suffered terribly – but she did an awful thing in writing it down for Rahul to find. If it's not wickedness, it's weakness: the inability to carry your own shit. So Claire offloaded it to Rahul, and here he was gifting it to me. Second-hand guilt, twice removed. That's what it all came down to – the circle of guilt and absolution. You can dance all you want, but there's no escaping the juggernaut.

"Did she know she'd die?" Rahul wanted to know. I was still calculating whether there was any other way out of this. Hollowness stretched inside me like a yawn. I said I didn't know and he asked me again:

"Do you think she knew all those awful things – what we did to her? Did she know she'd die?"

"We all die, Rahul."

"Did she know the day and hour of it? And still go out there and wait for it to happen? Did she watch for the car on the corner and not even move out of the way?"

Yes, that was another, more literal juggernaut. I was tired, and not just because day was creeping up behind the curtains.

"What do you want from me?" This was the where the night was heading – where it had always been heading. Who needs second sight to intuit the obvious?

Rahul carried the bottle to the car and propped it on the passenger seat, from where I'd be able to drag it into my flat. By a twist of fate I lived on the ground floor.

He put his hand on the window.

"You're my oldest friend. I didn't know who else to ask."

I pulled away from the kerb without replying. I saw him in the wing mirror; standing on the pavement in his torn slippers. Dawn broke behind him, a fiery hell putting the stars to flight. It was, momentarily, magnificent.

It took three and a half minutes to smash the bottle, and the greater part of the weekend to make sense of the notes and their fractured timeline.

I tacked each one to a wall, transforming the flat into an incident room. In turn the wall became an exploded portrait of a dead woman, a history told in a broken spiral.

It's funny how the past and future loop in on each other – that they're the same thing depending on where you're standing. Claire supposedly saw the future, but reading her predictions years later was like piecing together a diary. These were things that happened, once; they were dead events, done deals.

The notes gave flesh to her life and existence across one short decade, between the time we all met at university and until shortly before her death. There was nothing before that period, and there was nothing after it. That brief window of time makes sense if you think of the notes as a series of predictions — or a message — for someone who was only part of her life for those nine years. And of course she couldn't have predicted events after her death: that wouldn't be scrying the future, it would be beating God at his own game.

Rahul phoned several times, each attempt banked in the answering machine until I deleted the messages unheard.

I called him back on Tuesday, and he sounded like a bullied boy.

"Well?"

"If Claire knew how and when she'd die, she didn't write it down."

"Thank God. What else did she say?"

"Nothing of great importance to me. Private things. Things I shouldn't have read."

"I'm sorry." He trailed off, then picked up again mid-thought. "About us?"

It was a bright morning, and the shape of the window was cast in shadow on the back wall. I traced my finger over the cross where the frames intersected.

"She didn't know."

I heard him gulp and bury it in the back of his throat.

"Thank you," he said. "You don't know –'

"I have to go. I'll drop the notes back later."

He was still talking when I hung up.

I ate a sandwich and threw Claire's notes into a cardboard box. Not all of them, of course — some I ripped into tiny pieces and tossed among the eggshells and empty jars. They were the few notes that referred to "you and Rahul", and the single entry that was a letter from the past to the future. This one wasn't a prediction, but a hope. It was addressed to that same nameless "you", and it bestowed Rahul like you'd pass on an antique clock or your grandmother's wedding dress.

It was noon, but the car was covered in ice as thick as a penny. I filled the kettle again and, while it was tutting away, found myself searching through a drawer. I pulled out a notepad and turned to the first blank page. I stood looking down at it for some time. It was pristine on the face of it, but gouged with the marks of every page that had gone before: shopping lists and reminders and chimney stacks of numbers. I rolled the pen between my fingers before committing the thought, and then I wrote:

*January 12, 1999: the last time Rahul and I meet.*

I ripped the page out, folded it twice, and tucked it at the back of the drawer. I'd finish it later; I'd finesse it. It was, like any prediction, a meeting point of past, present and future. It was intent – and that is a beginning of sorts.

www.ingramcontent.com/pod-product-compliance
Lightning Source LLC
Chambersburg PA
CBHW030602130626
46552CB00006B/2632